Praise for *Dead Relatives*

'Macabre and menacing, I loved ev[...]
– Heidi James, *The Sound Mirr[...]*

'These gorgeous and horrible stories will break your heart and stamp on the pieces. Further proof that Lucie McKnight Hardy is one of the most exciting names in horror today.'
– Kylie Whitehead, *Absorbed*

'Eerie in many different and unexpected ways, Dead Relatives is full of strangeness, cold brutality and creeping dread. Tense and unforgettable.'
– Alice Ash, *Paradise Block*

"Lucie McKnight Hardy's writing is compulsively and exquisitely horrifying."
– Naomi Booth, *Exit Management*

"Raw, dark, disturbing…Lucie McKnight Hardy [is] a fabulous writer, subtle and playful and unswerving, and this anthology is utterly compelling, filled with intimate horrors, and unforgettable monsters."
– Amanda Mason, *The Hiding Place*

"Sensory, tactile and terrifying…Lucie McKnight Hardy can captivate with a single sentence."
– Stephen Volk, *Ghostwatch* **and** *Afterlife*

Praise for *Water Shall Refuse Them*

"Expertly juxtaposing folk horror and everyday reality, this impressive debut conveys an atmosphere of imminent menace."
– *The Guardian*

"A coming of age story where the threat of violence shimmers like a heat haze."
– Andrew Michael Hurley, *The Loney*

Also by Lucie McKnight Hardy

Water Shall Refuse Them

Dead Relatives

and other stories

LUCIE McKNIGHT HARDY

dead ink

dead ink

The right of Lucie McKnight Hardy to be identified as the
author of this work has been asserted by her in accordance
with the Copyright, Designs and Patents Act 1988.

First published in Great Britain in 2021 by Dead Ink,
an imprint of Cinder House Publishing Limited.

Every effort has been made to trace copyright holders within
the Hugh Sykes Davies estate to obtain permission for the
use of the quote within the epigraph.

Print ISBN 978-1-911585-82-4
Ebook ISBN 978-1-911585-83-1

Editing by Ella Chappell / reedsy.com/ella-chappell
Proofreading by Dan Coxon / momuseditorial.co.uk
Cover design by Luke Bird / lukebird.co.uk
Typeset by Laura Jones / lauraflojo.com

Printed and bound in Great Britain by TJ Books

www.deadinkbooks.com

Contents

For Cath and Karen,
and to dancing with Jimmy Corkhill at Casa's

in the stumps of old trees where the hearts have rotted out there are deep holes and dank pools where the rain gathers, and if you ever put your hand down to see, you can wipe it in the sharp grass till it bleeds, but you'll never want to eat with it again.

From 'Poem ("in the stump of the old tree…")', Hugh Sykes Davies

Contemporary Poetry and Prose, 7 (Nov. 1936), p. 129.

Dead Relatives

I

The Ladies are coming today and Cook is beside herself with worry.

'I'm beside myself with worry, Iris,' she says, and the blade strips the darkness from the backs of my eyes. 'Do not just sit there, Iris,' she says, turning the corpse over on the wooden board, spreading the legs just so. 'Go and find your mammy and ask her what jobs there are for you to do.' She drops the knife and her hand goes out for the cleaver.

But I don't go and find Mammy. Mammy – I know because I saw her, and her sherry bottle – is in her bedroom, having one of her rests, and so I stay sitting on the stool. The skin around my thumbnail is sore and tastes of coins. I hate Cook. I hate her lazy eye and her mean way with the gravy. I hate the way her bosom fills her apron, and I hate the way she looks at me, all pitying but still angry.

Cook brings the cleaver down on the neck – chop! – and the head comes off neatly, like slicing through blancmange.

It's the feet next – chop-chop-chop-chop – and they fall away, dainty as a babby's. The next bit is my favourite. She hooks her fingers around one of the legs and pushes on the stump of bone with her thumbs. The leg just slips out – pop! – like taking off a jacket. She works her way around the corpse, easing and tugging and pulling, and then, when all the legs are out, she gives a God-almighty heave and the whole skin comes off in one piece. It's like one of the Ladies taking off her fur coat. A fur coat with a red silk lining. That makes me smile.

Cook slings the scraps into the bucket and pushes aside the plastic strips that make a curtain through to the pantry, her fat arse slap-sliding all the way. I grab one of the tiny furry feet and slide it into the pocket of my pinafore, and I'm out of there, through the back door, quicker than a whippet from a trap.

Clippety Pete is getting the car out of the stable when I walk around the side of the house. He's funny, is Clippety Pete. It's only me who calls him that, and then it's only in my head. He got shrapnel stuck in his knee during the War and it's given him a limp. Clippety-cloppety Pete. Mammy doesn't like him, either. Got a face on him like a slapped arse, I heard her saying to Cook once, but that doesn't stop Cook from making eyes at him and sticking her titties out whenever he's about. He staggers out of the car, dragging his bad leg behind him. When he sees I'm watching him, he looks angry and pulls out a handkerchief and starts rubbing away at the bonnet. The grey paintwork stays just as dull and flat.

Dead Relatives

His dog is snuffling around at his feet: a terrier bitch, recently whelped, her teats are damp and bloated and red. They hang so low that they scrape along the ground as she potters along, and small bits of gravel cling to them. Suddenly, Clippety Pete straightens up and looks at me. He's sneering, like he's smelling something really bad. He has two fleshy mounds above his eyebrows that make him look as though he's frowning, even when he's not. But he is now.

'What you starin' at?' he says, but I just smile sweetly like butter wouldn't melt. That makes him look away. He's got even more grumpy since that bastard Beeching closed the station in the village, and he has to go into town now to collect the Ladies.

'How many of them are there this time?' I ask. Sometimes we have three, sometimes four, and once we even had five, but Mammy said that was too much trouble – never again.

'Three,' he mutters. He has to answer me because I am the heir to the house, the one who will inherit all this when Mammy's gone. Not that I wish her any ill. I skip away from him, and look back over my shoulder. Mammy makes him wear a tweed jacket when he goes to collect the Ladies, to make him look smart, but it's old and worn and the elbows are rubbed almost bare. He's put the handkerchief away and he's scratching away at his head – scritch-scritch-scritch – and I wonder if he has lice like I had last year. I loved the feeling of the tickly little buggers running through my hair, and the feel of their tiny feet on my scalp. Sometimes, if I was quick, I could catch one in my fingers and drag it out through the strands of my hair and it would crunch ever so slightly between my front teeth, like a biscuit crumb. I was sad when Mammy made Cook sit with me for hours, combing and combing and combing away, until they were all gone.

Clippety Pete's looking uncomfortable now. I can tell he wants to get on, to get to the railway station on time. If he's late the Ladies will be sure to ask the stationmaster to telephone the house like the last time and all hell will break loose when Mammy finds out. I decide to be nice to him and give him a nod to tell him he can leave. He grunts and gets into the Austin Traveller and slams the door louder than he needs to. As he sets off down the drive I give him a little curtsey and show him my teeth.

The dead tree is behind the garage, past the little pond and the greenhouse, and along the path. Everything's a bit ramshackle in the garden these days. There's moss all over the stable roof and the pond is dark and dank and covered in slimy green sludge; any fish in there have long since stopped swimming. The greenhouse is mildewed and the glass panes are either cracked or missing. It used to be a beautiful garden, with rose bushes and rhododendrons, and when I was little I used to run in between the laurel hedges, and make posies out of the convolvulus and camellias and primulas. There are no flowers this late in the year, and the hedges are wild and unruly since Jenkins the gardener left, all of a sudden, one day last winter. Didn't give us any warning, just left one night and didn't come back the next day, and Clippety Pete refused to do anything in the garden, saying his thumbs were proper pink, not green.

Dead Relatives

It's mizzling now, a grey-damp cloud hanging in the sky, and the dead tree looks even more withered and frail. It's a silver birch tree, I think – *Betula pendula* – but it's difficult to be sure because it no longer has any leaves and the tell-tale paper-like bark is just black now and flat. It's about six feet taller than me and leans at a slight angle, as though it's tired. I pull the corpse foot from the pocket of my pinafore and it leaves a little trail of blood on the fabric, and I know that Mammy's going to skin me (ha!) when she finds out, but I don't care as I have another feed for the tree. The hole in the bottom of the stump, where the heart has rotted out, is gaping, like a mouth, like a babby's mouth waiting for food. In goes the rabbit foot, into the hole, and I pinch some dirt in over it to cover it up. It disappears.

The garden lies quiet, as if it's sleeping. Nothing grows this late in November, and everything is sad and grey. The only thing of beauty is the lake that lies at the bottom of the slope, glittering and winking in the last of the sunlight. I trudge back to the house. I must prepare for the arrival of the Ladies.

There are eighteen steps to get to the half-landing, and then another six. At the top there they are, my dead relatives, all huddled together. It is gloomy on the landing, and Mammy makes sure to keep the curtains closed when there are going to be Ladies in the house, so I have to peer at my ancestors' faces to make sure they're in a friendly mood.

'Afternoon, Nanna Charlotte,' I say and give the old woman a little salute.

'Afternoon, Iris,' I think she says, and she gives me a tiny wink.

It's Auntie Maude next, and she's beaming her lovely smile. Little Vera, dead of smallpox at the age of eight, is grinning wildly, and Great Auntie Sarah frowns over her high-necked blouse. I work my way through all of them in turn, returning their smiles, nods and winks, their frowns and the tilts of their chins, mirroring their expressions, until I come to Granny Violet. I always leave Granny Violet to last. She's Mammy's mammy, and even though she was dead before I was born and so I never met her, I like to think that she wasn't as stern as she looks.

When I've finished my rounds, I stand back and address them all. 'We're having new Ladies today,' I tell them, and they all seem to look brighter. 'I'll make sure to introduce you.' And I think that Nanna Charlotte nods in assent. In the gloom, the birds and fish seem to bristle and flex their approval.

I walk down the corridor to my room, but go into the bathroom first. Mammy says we're the only people in the area to have an indoor bathroom and most other people in our village have to piss in the outhouse and I think that's funny, although Mammy doesn't say piss, she says urinate. I scrub my hands with the brush to get the dirt out from under my fingernails and then I take a facecloth to the smear of blood from the corpse foot but it just makes it spread and go brighter red, so I take my pinafore off and hide it in the pile of laundry in the corner waiting to be washed by Cook.

In my bedroom, Dolly's sitting on the end of my bed. She's not allowed to leave my room when there are Ladies in the house. Mammy says she might upset them, and it's true –

there's nothing pretty about Dolly. Her body's OK, nothing wrong with that, but her face is a bit wrong.

'New Ladies today, Dolly,' I whisper, and I think for a moment that her lopsided mouth tilts upwards. I give her a hug, and it's as though she hugs me back, and we're lying there, cuddling, when I hear the sound of the Austin Traveller crackling along the gravel drive.

From my bedroom window, I can just about see down to the steps that lead up to the front door, even though the top step is covered by the portico. The lead which covers it is pitted and curling and the summer's wisteria is still there, brown and parched and withered like the tops of Cook's titties. I can see the top of Clippety Pete's head, grey-brown strands greased over the bald patch that's not quite hidden by his floppy quiff, as he climbs up the steps, a suitcase in each hand. He disappears under the portico. Then one of the Ladies appears. Even from this angle, I can tell that she's tall, taller even than Pete, and broad, her shoulders set at a fair distance from each other. She has white-blonde hair piled up on the top of her head, none too neatly either, and from up here I can see black roots just about poking through. It makes me think of the photo of that woman – Myra somebody – one of the Ladies had shown me last year, in the newspaper she'd brought with her. I don't know why she was so famous, but the Lady told me Myra had done something dreadfully wicked, and I remember saying she had pretty eyes and Mammy got cross when I said that and threw the newspaper on the fire.

The blonde Lady disappears under the portico, and two other Ladies appear behind her, but I don't stay to watch. I give Dolly a kiss, pull a clean pinafore on over my head and run to the top of the stairs.

From where I stand, peering over the banister, I can just about see them as they step into the hall. Cook is there, doing a stupid curtsey in the black and white outfit Mammy makes her wear for the first day the Ladies arrive. Clippety Pete has dragged the suitcases into the hall, and the blonde Lady is standing next to him, taking her gloves off and looking around her. She's got thick, pale pink lips and lots of black stuff around her eyes. The other two Ladies step in after them. One is very thin, with hollow cheeks and straight dark hair. The other, her flushed face rimmed by a froth of mousy curls, is hefting along her own suitcase, bending over and huffing with the effort. Cook looks daggers at Pete, shoos the Lady away and takes the suitcase herself. All the luggage is placed in a neat pile at the bottom of the stairs. The Ladies are ushered into the drawing room by Cook, and I know that she will be telling them to sit down and make themselves comfortable. It's the same every time. We have a routine, almost a performance, and Mammy gets cross if we deviate from it.

'Sluts.' Sometimes, words just land in my mouth like pebbles. They bounce around for a while and then they tumble out. It's as though I don't have any control over them. I think they come from my dead relatives. I think they're telling me what to say, on their behalf, and I can't stop myself. I remember once, when Mammy and Cook were talking, and Mammy said she thought one of the Ladies was haughty, and Little Vera popped into my head and made me say, 'Does that mean she's a whore?' and the slap came from nowhere, stinging my ear for a week. This time, I think it's Great Auntie Sarah who's responsible. I stare into her eyes, and she stares back, but she's smirking, challenging me. I tiptoe down the stairs.

The door is not quite shut, and I can see the blonde Lady, slivered by the crack, settled onto the sofa. She is robust and butter-skinned and plump like an oyster. She takes a golden powder compact from her handbag and dabs at her nose, assessing herself in the mirror. She must like what she sees, because she gives a little pouty smile and puts the compact away.

'Iris!' Cook says, striding out of the drawing room. It makes me jump and my heart goes bang-bang-bang. 'Iris Alice Sefton, stop peeking at keyholes. It is not becoming in a young lady.' I think about telling Cook that I'm not peeking at keyholes, I'm peering through cracks, but she's already making for the kitchen, her fat old arse bouncing after her. I'm watching her go, the two loaves of her bum rubbing together, when she swings back round and gives me a sharp nod, and that is the signal for me to make my entrance.

They all look up at me when I go in, and they all smile, expectantly. They're still wearing their coats and all sitting the same way – ankles close together, hands clasped onto their handbags which are sitting on their laps, as though someone's arranged them, like dolls. I give them the full benefit of my grin, and the skinny one, who is sitting with her back to the fireplace, is the first to look away, the smile sliding off her face when she realises I'm not like them. I'm more like Dolly.

'Mama will be here soon,' I say in the voice Mammy has made me practise to use in front of the Ladies. They nod and look away and down at their hands, all except for the blonde Lady who keeps on looking at me. She has a kind face, despite all the make-up. Mammy says make-up is for slatterns. I can hear Clippety Pete out in the hall. He's bringing in the luggage and the sound of him dragging his leg behind him is funny. I put a hand up to cover my mouth, because Mammy says it is uncouth to smile to oneself. Besides, there's my teeth to think about. And there's still soil under my nails and my knuckles are grubby, despite my efforts earlier. Quickly, I hide my hands behind my back, and it's a good thing, too, because that's when Mammy comes in and it's like the air is sucked out of the room.

All the women tense, but none of them stand up. She has that effect on people, always has done. Mammy's tall, see, like a man, and she's got broad shoulders and big hands. She keeps her hair cut short and has ruddy cheeks and hairs sprouting from her chin. I even overheard Cook joking to Clippety Pete one day that Mammy might have been a man in disguise and I laughed and laughed and laughed at that, because where did I come from if not from the womb of Mammy? She's wearing her best dress, the green one that finishes below the knee and has a wide collar, and she looks regal.

'Good afternoon, ladies. Welcome to Bank House,' she says, and even her voice is deep and commanding. The Ladies nod. The blonde one is looking at Mammy, but the other two are looking down into their laps. I think they must be shy.

'We all know why we're here,' Mammy says, starting the same speech she gives every time we have Ladies to stay. 'Cook – whom I believe you have already met – will show you to your rooms on the second floor. You will unpack and then we will meet for dinner at six o'clock sharp. Cook will ring the dinner bell. I realise that in your... condition, you may not be hungry at meal times, but it is expected that you will

eat at regular intervals, so there will be no skipping meals.
Now. Is that clear?'

Like meek little schoolgirls, two of the Ladies nod again,
but the blonde one just looks at Mammy. Her eyes are
narrowed slightly and her lips are twisted into a very small
smile. Clippety Pete is shuffling around in the hall with the
luggage. Mammy claps her hands and the Ladies startle.
'Come on, then. Let's get moving,' Mammy says, and as
the Ladies stand up and start to walk towards the door I am
happy to see their bellies.

Lovely, smooth, round bellies, gently swelling under their
coats. Each with a little babby in it.

The bones are tiny, sharp flashes of white against the brown.
Mammy's having none of it, and she makes Cook take the
stew back out to the kitchen.

'Make sure you inspect it good and proper,' she says.
'People could choke on them.'

The Ladies shift in their seats and look uncomfortable. The
mousy one – Miss Eccles – is sitting next to me, toying with
her cutlery, pushing the blade of the knife in between the tines
of the fork. She looks up and sees me watching her and I give
her one of my best smiles, but she looks away again, blushing
furiously. I think she might be about to cry. The blonde one
– Miss Haddon – seems bolder and she starts drumming her
nails, ever so softly, on her water glass. Mammy shoots her a
look and she stops, but when she sees me looking at her she
gives me a little nod, so I nod back. Then she nods back at
me, so I do the same and there we are, me and the blonde

Lady, giving each other tiny little nods until Cook comes back in with the stew. She puts it on the table with a slop and gives the back of Mammy's head a hard stare, like she wants to fry her brains. Mammy peers into the stew pot.

'Ah, yes, that's better,' she says, and starts to ladle the brown stuff onto her plate. She passes the pot to the Lady on her left – Miss Riley, the skinny one – and Miss Riley takes the pot and puts it down on the table next to her. She's small-boned and delicate, like a little bird, and her wrists are tiny and look as though they might snap from the weight of the ladle as she lifts it out of the pot and places a minute amount of stew on her plate.

'Ah, come on now, girl!' says Mammy, and she takes the ladle from her and dumps a huge clod of the brown stuff down. 'Eat up. You need to keep your strength up.' She pokes the Lady under the ribs, none too gently, either. 'There's nothing to you, to be sure.'

Miss Riley looks as though she's going to throw up, and I grab the stew pot off the table before she can be sick into it. I twirl the ladle around in it, just in case Cook has left another stray bone in there, but there's nothing except chunks of rabbit and carrots and brown sauce. I pull out a few lumps of the meat and then I pass the pot to Miss Eccles. And so it goes, round the table, and we all help ourselves and some of us eat more than others. No-one says very much, but Mammy is watching us all over her spectacles, and more than once my eyes meet with those of the blonde Lady, and we share a little smile.

When we have all finished (and I suspect Miss Riley has hidden her meat in her napkin), Cook comes and clears the dishes. I know that she and Clippety Pete are meant to share the leftovers, but I also know that Cook will have hidden some of the better bits of meat in the scullery before she's brought the pot out to the dining room.

Mammy lets the Ladies sit in the drawing room after dinner. They each sit on the chair they took when they arrived, and I wonder if that's going to be their chair for the whole time they're with us. That's usually the way. Mammy hasn't said how long they'll be here this time, but judging by their bellies, I'd say a good couple of months. They will all go to bed soon; Mammy says that, in their condition, they should be getting lots of rest. They all have their own rooms on the top floor, each with a piss pot and a paraffin lamp, because even though we've got electricity and plumbing, it doesn't go all the way up there. Mammy says it's where the servants used to sleep, all the way up at the top of the house, and I try to think of Cook lugging her fat arse up all those steps every night. It's better, I think, that she sleeps in the little parlour behind the kitchen. Sometimes, so does Clippety Pete, but I don't think Mammy knows about that.

Cook's gone to feed the chickens, so I go into the kitchen. I get tangled in the plastic strips of the pantry doorway, like I always do, but I don't mind because it feels like seaweed and I'm a mermaid. It's Stir-up Sunday, and there's a big bowl of dried fruit soaking in sherry on the side; it smells like Mammy's breath. In the scraps bowl there's a handful of the tiny white bones that Mammy made Cook pick out of the stew earlier, and I take them out, one by one. I hold one up to my eye and squint at it. It's curved, and I can see creamy-white here and there through the slime of the stew. I look them all over carefully and give them a wipe on my sleeve and slip them into the pocket of my pinafore. Then I pirouette and step, mermaid-like, back through the seaweed.

Cook's back in the kitchen, scrubbing at the plates.

'What are you doing in there, Iris?' she says. 'I hope you ain't up to no good.' I flash her my teeth. She flinches and looks up at the clock on the wall. 'Go and tell the Ladies to go upstairs,' she says, and the bubbles fluff up around her wrists. 'Time for them to go to bed.'

I watch her for a minute, her fleshy forearms rubbing at the plates, the tops of her arms jiggling away, and I think of the time I saw her and Clippety Pete in the parlour, but that time it was his flabby arse cheeks that were jiggling away in between her lumpy thighs and she was going, 'Ooh, ooh, ooh.'

In the drawing room, the Ladies are all sitting in their chairs. Miss Riley's next to the window, and she's staring out, despite it being pitch black out there, and not a thing to be seen. She's gnawing away on a fingernail. Miss Eccles is next to the fireplace, hunkered up next to it, even though the fire hasn't been lit. She's got a pile of wool in her lap, grey and coiled like a rat, and her knitting needles are clicking away. She doesn't look up. The blonde Lady is lounging on the settee. She's taken her shoes off and tucked her feet under her, and her dress has rucked up around her thighs, which, even through her nylons, I can see are meaty and strong. Her belly's pushing up through the material and there's a magazine perched on top of it.

I stand in the middle of the room, and address them all at once.

'Time for you to go to bed, Ladies,' I say.

Dead Relatives

Miss Riley turns from the window, her eyebrows raised in indignation. I suspect she's not used to having a thirteen-year-old tell her when her bedtime is. Miss Eccles mutters something about just finishing another couple of rows, and her knitting needles clack away with urgency. The blonde Lady closes her magazine and, with a bit of an effort, swings her feet off the sofa and onto the floor. She slides her feet into her shoes and smiles up at me.

'Thank you, Iris. Any chance you could help me up?'

'Yes, Miss Haddon,' I say.

'Nancy. Please call me Nancy. I feel like an old woman when people call me Miss Haddon.' I take her hand and pull and at the same time she pushes herself up from the sofa. She doesn't let go of my hand, so I lead the way out into the hall and up the stairs and she follows me, hoisting her knees up in front of her like she's climbing bloody Mount Everest or something, but then I think of the babby in her belly, and how it must be weighing her down.

We get to the landing and it's gloomy. She stands there for a moment, getting her breath back, her hands pressed into her back. I open the curtains, even though Mammy has said I mustn't. There's a full moon and it's just about bright enough to make out my dead relatives.

She takes her time looking at them, squinting at them all in turn, getting right up close, and I think they are a bit disapproving. Auntie Maude is frowning, and Little Vera is positively gurning her distaste, but Nancy doesn't seem bothered by this; she just keeps on peering.

'Who are all these people, then, Iris?' Nancy asks, as if she knows I've been bursting to tell her. 'Are they your relatives?'

She doesn't wait for me to answer. 'Her: she's a serious soul, isn't she?' She's looking at Nanna Charlotte, and Nanna Charlotte's glowering right back. I don't think I've ever seen her so cross.

'They're Mammy's ancestors,' I say, and I think Nanna Charlotte's frown relaxes slightly.

'There's a lot of them,' Nancy says, and she's right; the whole wall is covered in photographs, some black-and-white, some sepia.

'It's Mammy. She says we should remember the dead, particularly our relatives. Keep them close to us.' A flicker of a frown touches Nancy's forehead, and then it's gone again. 'They've all lived in this house, ever since it was built more than two hundred years ago.'

Nancy straightens up. 'It's a big house,' she says. 'Must have been full of people in the olden days.' She's right. I've heard Cook and Clippety Pete saying how the house is too big for just me and Mammy and that Mammy should sell it and get somewhere smaller, but I know Mammy would never do that. There's history here, she would say, and history should be respected.

I point to the glass cases that sit on top of the bookshelves next to the window, and Nancy goes over to them, peers into their murky interiors.

'Birds?' she says. 'Is that what they are? Stuffed birds.'

I nod, although, really, it's bloody obvious. There are at least a dozen of them, all different shapes and sizes.

'Taxidermied,' I say, proud of being the keeper of that word. 'It's Clipp— Peter,' I tell her. 'He traps them on the lake and stuffs them. He's got a workshop in the stable and he's been doing it for years. He wasn't very good at first – you can see, those ones at the back are all lopsided and their feet are funny – but he reckons he's really good now. Mammy lets him keep them here so they're not cluttering up the drawing room.' It's the most I've said in ages, and I have to stop and draw a breath.

Nancy's frowning, but not in a bad way. More like she's confused.

'There's all sorts there,' I bluster on. 'Look, that one at the back's a great crested grebe – *Podiceps cristatus* – and that little one, with the orange head and the stripe down its face, that's *Anas falcata* – a falcated teal.'

Nancy raises her eyebrows. I can feel myself blush, and I give a silent thanks to G.F. Faulkner's *The Birds of Britain and Europe*.

'Well, Iris, that's very impressive,' she says, and even though I think she's being a bit patronising, I can't help feeling proud. 'Did you learn all that at school?'

I shake my head. 'I don't go to school. I never have. Mammy says it's a waste of time. I teach myself.'

'You teach yourself?' She repeats it as a question, and I nod and point at the bookshelves.

'I read lots. Dictionaries, encyclopaedias, that sort of thing. Reference books. Mammy says I'm like a sponge, soaking it all up.'

'Well, you've certainly got a good memory.' I feel the colour rising in my cheeks again, and that's when I decide to show Nancy the pike. It's hidden at the back of the display, both because it's by far the biggest, and because Cook says it gives her the creeps. *Esox lucius* is about three feet long and has green speckles the colour of snot all along its flank. Six fins stick out, a bit like hands, along its side, and every time I look at it, I can imagine those hands wafting through the darkness at the bottom of the lake, propelling it along as it hunts for prey. The worst thing about the pike, though, is its mouth. Clippety Pete has mounted it so that its jaws are wide open in a snarl, showing off its teeth. There are tiny ones, no bigger than a babby's fingernail, but sharp as razors, and there are bigger ones that stick up here and there, and look like they'd be enough to take your hand off.

I used to have nightmares about the pike, and would wake up sweating, fighting the beast off me, drowning in the lake water, and then I would have to snuggle up really close to Dolly before I could go back to sleep.

Nancy pays the pike no heed, other than to wrinkle her nose a bit and frown.

'I'm going to go to bed now, Iris. It's been a long day and I'm knackered.'

I decide that I like Nancy. I like her very much.

I wake up and the morning is cold and early-blue. Dolly is lying next to me, and I have my arm around her neck. I hug her close to me.

I can hear Cook clattering about in the kitchen, making breakfast. I get out of bed and go to the bathroom, pull my knickers down and sit on the toilet. My piss is bright yellow and lovely and warm, and there's a rising trail of steam. I think of Nancy, up in her attic room, and how pretty she looked as she slept last night, lying on her back, her hands clasped over her belly, like a carved saint on a tomb. Prettier than the other Ladies. There's ice on the inside of the window in my bedroom, and I use my finger to draw a vertical line, then a diagonal one, and then another vertical line. 'N' for Nancy.

Downstairs, they're already in the dining room. There's a big pan of grey porridge and some boiled eggs in a bowl on the sideboard. Nobody is eating. Nancy looks up at me and smiles, but the other two – Miss Riley and Miss Eccles – avoid my eye and look at their plates. I can hear Cook in the kitchen, wheezing and shuffling, and then there's the sharp whistle of the kettle boiling and Miss Eccles near jumps out of her skin. Her hand goes up to her chest and she holds it there for a moment, before letting out a long breath. Nancy and I share a smile.

When Cook brings the tea into the room, everyone perks up a bit. She pours it, steaming, into cups and passes them round, then plonks a sugar bowl and a milk jug on the table. Nancy is the first to help herself, and this seems to encourage Miss Eccles, as she grins nervously and copies Nancy. Miss Riley drinks her tea without milk or sugar.

After slurping noisily, Nancy hoists herself to her feet and goes to the sideboard. She stands for ages, as if she's not sure what to eat, even though there are only two choices. Eventually she lumps some porridge into a bowl and goes to sit back down again, easing herself into the chair nice and slow. She reaches for the sugar bowl, and, quicker than a rat in a trap, Cook's there and slaps her hand away. It's the same every time.

'No sugar – only salt on porridge,' she snaps. 'Mistress's orders.' She always smirks when she says this, her thin lips making two tiny crevices into the fleshy domes of her cheeks. Nancy flushes for a second, then she shrugs and, ignoring the salt cellar, puts a spoonful of the grey porridge into her mouth. She carries on looking Cook right in the eye, chews a couple of times and then swallows, raises her eyebrows. Cook glares at her, then turns and clomps back to the kitchen. I like Nancy even more now.

I choose a boiled egg from the bowl on the sideboard, even though they're barely still warm. I like tapping on the top to make the shell crinkle and break, and then scraping it back to reveal the egg inside, never seen by anyone other than me. I break apart the white and there's a blood spot on top of the yolk. This is a sign that today is a good day, and I scoop it up and swallow it whole.

After breakfast is always the time when the Ladies must go and have a private talk with Mammy in the little cupboard she calls the office. The door doesn't shut properly, and it's easy to hear what is being said if you sit on the fifth stair up from the bottom.

'How far gone are you?' asks Mammy in her official voice. There's a pause, and then someone – either Miss Eccles or Miss Riley, I can't tell because they've hardly uttered a single bloody word since they've been in the house – mutters something.

'Speak up, girl!' Mammy can be mean.

'I don't know. About seven months or so.' There's a pause, and a rustling of clothing.

'More than that, if you ask me,' Mammy says roughly. 'But you'll be the better judge of that.' I can hear the sneer in her voice. 'Now, do you have something for me?' Again, silence except for a rustle – this time of paper, and then a fanning sound, and I know Mammy is counting the money. 'Good. Everything is in order. Now, make yourself comfortable. You'll be here for a good few weeks, so best you settle in.'

I jump to my feet and pretend to be walking down the stairs as Miss Eccles comes out. Her pink cheeks are even pinker than usual, and she won't look at me. She's blinking back tears, her hair foaming around her face.

Mammy makes it clear to the Ladies before they arrive that she has already found parents to take on their babbies: barren couples who are desperate for a child to cherish and dote on. She shows them the advertisements she places in the London papers, asking for *devoted parents for unfortunate children*. They've already seen the other advertisements she's placed: *'Attention: women in a delicate situation seeking accommodation. Bed and board available and solutions to predicaments procured. Apply box number...'* It's a hidden language, all suggestions and insinuations and such, but everyone knows what it means.

I pull my coat on and open the front door, lifting it slightly on its hinges to stop it from squeaking. I know all the tricks. It's colder today than it was yesterday, and the sky is flat and blank. There's not even a wind to ruffle the surface of the lake, just the dull ache of winter. Cook lit the fire in the drawing room after breakfast and the Ladies had settled themselves in: Nancy with her magazine, Miss Eccles with her bright pink cheeks and her ever-growing mound of grey knitting, and Miss Riley, scribbling away on a sheet of writing paper and occasionally gazing out, unblinking, through the window.

I duck down as I leave the house, in case she should see me as I pass her window and ask where I'm going. Truth be told, she seems a bit scared of me, which is fair, I suppose, given my appearance. She had the same meeting with Mammy as Miss Eccles did after breakfast, except she came out, after handing over the money, with her jaw set firm and her eyes hard and glassy.

The milk jug makes a lump in my pocket, and I have to walk very carefully to get to the dead tree without spilling any. There's been a fine covering of snow overnight – not enough to make the garden look pretty, but just enough to make the grass slippery. My feet slide a little bit when I get to the greenhouse, and the milk makes a damp patch on my pinafore. The dead tree is exactly as I left it yesterday; if you didn't know what was in the hole you wouldn't give it another glance. I take the milk jug out of my pocket and reach into the dark hollow. It's awkward because the top of the hole is at ankle height, so I have to lean over and into it. It's warmer in the hole than it is outside, and I think that must be because of what it contains. Carefully, I pour the milk into the hole, a trickle of sustenance, and then I take the rabbit bones from my pocket and sprinkle them on top. The tree must be fed frequently or it will not thrive.

November has become December and the weather has turned colder still. Cook's mood has taken a turn for the worse as well, because Mammy insists that she keeps the fire stoked, and every evening she has to lug her big fat arse up to the attic rooms to put hot water bottles in the Ladies' beds. Clippety

Pete spends most of his time in the stable, working on his birds, and that makes Cook even crosser. She says he should bring in all the ducks and geese he traps because they're good for cooking with. Instead he brings her moorhens and coots, and she protests that there's no flesh on them.

The Ladies don't mention it, but I can tell they're getting restless as their bellies get bigger. Miss Eccles – Veronica, as Nancy calls her – has taken to wearing the enormous, shapeless grey jumper she's been knitting since she's been with us. When her hands aren't fidgeting away at her knitting needles, working on her new orange monstrosity, she pulls the sleeves down over her hands and curls up into her chair. Miss Riley just sits at the window, biting her fingernails to the quick until they bleed, sometimes scribbling away on her notepad, then tucking the sheets into envelopes.

It's just after lunch, and the light outside is beginning to fail. Mammy has got me and Nancy making paper chains. 'Idle hands make work for the devil,' she'd said, and that made me chuckle.

Nancy has big hands and long fingers, and she wears a ring on her wedding finger, but I know it's fake, because she told me.

'People can be awfully judgemental, Iris,' she said, when she saw me looking at the ring. 'Just because you're in the family way and not married, they look down on you; people think you're worse than they are.' She told me the ring was a cheap brass thing she'd bought in the market when her belly started to show. 'It stops people staring, you know.' And she pointed at her belly, which was straining mightily against her jumper.

The ring is glinting in the light from the fire as she threads the paper strips through each other and glues them together. Red and pink and orange, we've chosen – 'Nice and bright, Iris. This place could do with cheering up.' And at first Mammy looked a bit disapproving, but she didn't say anything. It's peaceful, sitting there with Nancy, threading the paper links through each other, until she does a great big dramatic sigh and puts the paper chain down and leans back on her hands.

'Oh, Iris,' she says. 'I'm so bloody bored. Is there nothing to do around here? A shop or anything? Somewhere I can get a new magazine? I've read that one a million times.' She gestures towards her copy of *Woman's Weekly*, with its orange and grey cover promising recipes for a cheese party platter and a dress pattern for 1s 6d. It's tatty and dog-eared now, the corners curling into themselves. I tell her that the nearest shop is in the village, three miles away, but I don't tell her that we never go there. Cook grows all our fruit and veg in the garden and the orchard, and then there's whatever birds and fish Clippety Pete gets from the lake, and the odd rabbit or hare. We've chickens, too, so a good supply of eggs, and if we're really running low, then Cook will go out and wring a neck or two. It means we very rarely have to go anywhere, except when what Mammy calls 'the staples' run low and she sends Pete to the shop in the next town where they don't know us. I don't tell Nancy that I've never left the grounds of Bank House.

She picks up the paper chain again and starts picking at it with her fingernails. 'And you don't even have a telly or a radio. I can't believe you can live like this, especially you, a teenager!' That makes me smile. I know what a teenager is, of course, even though we have no television or wireless. One of the Ladies who stayed here last year had left a magazine behind in her room and I found it before Cook went up to change the sheets. Teenager was one of those words that Mammy would never use: brash, modern, uncouth, she'd say. The magazine had made me marvel – lots of ladies with make-up and the most colourful, brazen clothing I'd ever seen. Some of them had skirts so short you could almost see what they'd had for breakfast, as Cook would say. I'd put the magazine on Clippety Pete's bonfire as soon as I'd read it. Mammy would have gone through the roof if she knew.

'Ow!' Nancy drops the paper chain she's threading and puts a finger in her mouth. She sucks on it for a moment, frowning, then takes it out and looks at it. 'Bloody paper cut.' She drops the strip of paper she's holding and I can see that there's a smear of blood on it, rusty against the orange. Her eyes flit to the window. Outside, the sky is a dull white. 'Tell you what, let's go for a walk. We can wander down to the lake and see what birds we can spot. You can tell me their posh names, if you like. And then we can pick some holly and ivy and make proper decorations when we get back.' She nudges the pile of coiled paper with her foot.

'Alright,' I say, 'but you'll need to wrap up warm. It looks as though it's going to snow.'

'Oh, Iris,' she says. 'You do mollycoddle me.' She rolls her eyes, but at the same time she's smiling. I feel glad.

She goes into the hall to get her coat, and I pick up the piece of paper with the bloodstain and crumple it into a ball in the palm of my hand. In the hall, Nancy's struggling into her coat. It doesn't button up anymore, so she just pulls the sides together over her belly and ties the belt. My coat is old, and the sleeves are too short for me, so I pull the sleeves of my cardigan down underneath them to cover my hands.

Outside, the cold is like a slap. We stand under the portico for a moment, and the air smells heavy with the threat of snow. On the gravelled parking area, Clippety Pete's bitch is snuffling about, looking for food. Her empty belly is sagging, and her teats trail along the ground, stirring up gravel.

'Oh, that poor dog,' says Nancy. 'What's the matter with it? It looks so… pathetic.'

'Not long whelped,' I say. 'She had six pups not long ago.'

'Puppies? Oh, Iris, do you think I could see them? Where are they? In the stable?'

'In the lake, more like.' And I can't help snorting a little bit.

Nancy's face drains. 'The lake? Why… What…?'

'We can't have pups, Mammy says. Six more mouths to feed. Pete put them in a sack with a load of stones and slung them in the lake.'

Nancy takes a sharp little breath inwards, and her eyes are watering. 'Oh, how very, very sad. That poor dog. She must be so miserable. Imagine losing your babies like that.' She has her hands resting on her belly, sort of covering it, protective. She's frowning, with her mouth as well as her forehead, but then all of a sudden she's smiling, her eyes wide.

'The baby, Iris! It's kicking. I've only felt it a couple of times before. I think it's saying it's almost ready to come out.'

I picture the tiny babby in her womb, its feet thrusting against the wall of her belly, its arms waving.

'What does it feel like?' I ask. 'You know – to have a babby in your belly?'

Nancy shrugs. 'It's uncomfortable. It's heavy and sometimes a little bit painful. But it's also wonderful – knowing
that I'm going to be bringing a new person into the world.
It's… I don't know… fulfilling, I suppose.'

I put my hand out. I want to feel the babby. Nancy takes
a step back, away from me.

'It's stopped now, Iris. I'll tell you next time it does that
and you can see if you can feel it.'

Then I see that I still have the piece of paper with her blood
on it in my outstretched hand, but Nancy hasn't noticed, so I
put it, carefully, into my coat pocket. I slide my arm through
Nancy's and she looks at me and pats my hand.

'Come on,' she says, and together we walk to the bottom
of the garden.

The path we walk along goes down towards the lake at a
shallow slope, hairpinning all the way down to the bottom
of the garden. We go past the little pond, and she insists
on stopping to look for fish, even though I know they're
long-dead, and then the greenhouse, with its broken panes
and mildew. And then we get to the dead tree. It looks
unremarkable, really, if you don't know how special it is, and
it seems even more dead today, black and gnarled against
the flat, white sky. I give the hole at the base of the tree a
quick glance, but there's nothing to see – the egg I'd taken
from the chicken house and broken in there yesterday has
disappeared completely, soaked into the mud and decaying
wood. Claimed as nourishment.

Even though you can see the lake from the top of the
hill, next to the house, by the time you get to the bottom of
the garden, the fruit cages there are so overgrown that they

obscure the lake until you're right next to it. Except it's not really a lake. Mammy insists we call it that, but really it's an old gravel pit they flooded when it went out of use. It's pretty, though – the water stretches away to the far bank, with a little island in the middle that's dotted with trees. I try not to think about the pike, down in the black depths of the lake, swimming, searching, with their razor-sharp teeth, for prey.

Nancy's blowing on her hands and stamping her feet. 'It's colder than it looks,' she says.

'Do you want to go back?' I ask.

She shakes her head. 'Not just yet. It's good to be outside, to get some fresh air.' The cold has brought a flush to her cheeks, and she looks beautiful, standing there, staring out over the water. She's taken to wearing her hair loose over her shoulders, rather than up in the elaborate style she told me was called a beehive, and it suits her. It makes her look younger, more innocent, even though her black roots are now a good inch long.

'It's beautiful here, isn't it?' Nancy says, not taking her eyes off the lake. 'I mean, there's nothing to do, and nowhere to go, but you're still lucky to live here, I reckon.'

I'd never thought about it like that before. I'd never once thought that there could ever be any other way of living. I'd always just accepted that this was my life and that it would continue and nothing would ever change. That I would carry on doing what Mammy does and one day I'd have a babby of my own, a little girl. All Sefton babbies are girls. Yes, the lake is beautiful, but there's always something lurking under the surface, in the dark.

'What's that, Iris?' she asks, and she's pointing to one of the leafless trees on the island. In it hangs a black shape, slim, almost vertical.

'*Phalacrocorax carbo*,' I tell her. 'A cormorant.'

'It's lovely, isn't it? So elegant.'

'Or it might be *Phalacrocorax aristotelis*,' I say, proud. 'It's difficult to tell them apart when they're roosting.'

'And what is that when it's at home?' she asks, smiling.

'A shag,' I say innocently enough, and she throws back her head and laughs.

'Oh, Iris, I can see that you and I are going to be good friends. I'm not actually that much older than you, I don't think.'

'I'm thirteen,' I say.

'Well, then. The difference is only six years. Do you know, I was dreading coming here. When I met Veronica and Peggy at the railway station, I thought them the dullest people I'd ever met and I didn't know how I was going to manage to stay here until the baby came. Now, I can pretend I'm your big sister.'

I nod, but I don't tell her that only Dolly will ever be my sister.

We walk back up to the house, slowly to allow for Nancy's bulky belly, and she stops halfway along the path at a clump of ivy that's growing up the trunk of an oak tree. She's stretching up to reach a long strand of the stuff and she has her back to me. Quickly, I dart over to the dead tree, and pull the crumpled up piece of paper chain from my coat pocket. Nancy's blood is still smeared across the surface. In it goes, into the hole, and I panic for a moment, as it sits there, bright orange against the dark interior. Then it slips, and falls out of view, as though it has been claimed.

Nancy has gathered an armful of ivy, and is standing, looking up at the house. 'It's massive, isn't it?' she says. 'There are big houses in London, but none of them on their own like this.' She's right. It's huge, three storeys, although the only sign of the attic rooms from outside is the tiny window on the gable end. For the first time I see it through someone else's eyes: the chipped red brick with the pointing falling away, the paint flaking on the window frames, the cracked panes that Clippety Pete has never got around to fixing. Even the portico, which should make it look grand and imposing, is leaning backwards slightly, as though it doesn't have the strength to stand upright.

'Do you live in a big house?' I ask Nancy, and she snorts.

'No, I live in a bedsit. I share it with a friend. We even have to share the bed.' I can feel my eyebrows lift and she smiles. 'It's not so bad. She works a night shift and I work days.' She catches herself. 'Of course, I don't now. That's the other thing. As soon as this baby's taken care of and I get back to London, I'll have to find another job.' She sighs. 'Shouldn't be too bad. I've got eighty words per minute typing and seventy shorthand.'

I decide not to tell her that I don't know what she's talking about.

Clippety Pete's bitch is still snuffling around when we get back up to the house. Nancy was right – it's a pathetic creature right enough. I'd watched it getting fatter and fatter over the weeks before it whelped, and then one day I found it at the back of the stable lying on its side and panting. After all my years of hearing the Ladies, I knew what was going to happen, and I knew I should go and get Pete, but I couldn't drag myself away, and eventually the bitch made a horrible keening noise and there was suddenly a slime of meat coming out the back of her. As I watched, another, then another pup slithered out, until six of them lay there, twitching and mewling. The bitch rolled around and started licking the stuff off them. I was still watching when she picked up one of the pups in her mouth and, instead of licking it, started chewing. She crunched it up between her molars, and swallowed the whole thing down. That's when I ran to get Pete.

I look at Nancy, and she's staring at the bitch, both hands resting on the curve of her belly. There's a veil of concern over her face and I decide I won't tell her what I saw. That's when I feel the first few flakes of snow licking my cheeks.

II

The snow came down heavily that evening, and it continued for the best part of a week. The garden took on a new, cosseted quality, as though the snow was blanketing not just the greenhouse and the hedges and the stone walls, but was keeping everything safe until spring could arrive.

Now, the garden lies flat and still, and it's all I can do to slip out of the house and get down to feed the dead tree. My feet leave tracks in the snow, big versions of those left by the rabbits and the hares desperately seeking food, and when I go out I have to make a tour of the garden so my footprints are everywhere so it's not obvious to Clippety Pete or Cook that I've been to visit the tree. It takes bloody ages.

There are great banks where the snow has drifted against the hedges, and Pete struggled yesterday to get the car out of the drive. I was watching him from the gable window high up in Nancy's bedroom, as the wheels spun round and round, and then they stopped turning altogether, and the car slipped back down the slope of the drive and staggered to a rest in the parking area. He tried again a couple of times, but in the end he gave up, dragged himself out of the car and slipped on the compacted snow, landing flat square on his arse. I laughed and called to Nancy to come and look, but she was pouting at herself in the mirror, putting her lipstick on, and by the time she'd pushed herself up off the bed, huffing and puffing, he was back on his feet again.

It's nice up in Nancy's room. She's made it cosy, with a pink silk scarf pinned up at the window, so the light is soft and gentle, even when outside it's harsh and brittle. It's cold up there, though, so we didn't stay long. Other than at meal times, when Mammy insists everyone is present in the dining room, Miss Riley – Peggy – has taken to sitting in her bedroom, with a great, thick blanket draped around her shoulders. She doesn't speak to anyone except when she has to, like when she hands Mammy a letter and asks her to post it. Veronica – Miss Eccles – sits in the drawing room all day, the clatter of her bloody knitting needles measuring out the length of the orange scarf she's taken to knitting. For her husband, she says, and that made Nancy snort into her hand. It's funny that they try to keep up the pretence like that. Veronica and Peggy both have fake wedding rings like Nancy's – cheap brass stuff that they fidget with. We all know why they're here, but the only one who's honest about it is Nancy.

When it gets too cold to sit in Nancy's bedroom, we sometimes sit on the landing. I can't take Nancy into my room because she might see Dolly, who sits in her rightful place on my pillow, so we've made a little corner of the landing into a den. I've taken cushions from the drawing room and arranged them in a half-circle and even added an electric blanket I found in Cook's parlour. I don't talk to my dead relatives when Nancy's with me – I think it would embarrass them – but they keep a watch over us and sometimes I catch them frowning. I don't think they like Nancy as much as I do.

'Do you mind if I do something with your hair?' Nancy says to me. We're sitting in the corner next to the window. She's been reading her magazine again, and pointing out some dresses to me, saying that she's going to save up and buy them after the baby comes and she's back at work. All the dresses are gaudy and short, and the ladies in the magazine are wearing high boots that come over their knees and I can't think how they could walk in them. Mammy would call them common. I've finished the ornithology books and the tree books and have started reading the dictionary again, beginning at random with 'H'. Nancy starts dragging her fingers through my hair, tugging my head back. 'You look like a wraith,' she says.

'Ow,' I say, but only because I think it's what she's expecting, not because it hurts. It's nice, in fact, to feel someone's fingers on me. She twists a string of my hair around a finger. 'Your hair is… silky,' Nancy says and I think then that she's not like all the rest, the other Ladies who have come and refuse to look at me. There's something of the devil about Nancy: she'll look him in the eye and kick him in the arse, as Cook would say.

'There, all done,' she says, and I put a hand up to my hair, all untangled and soft now.

Nancy takes my hands between hers and rubs them and she's smiling, but it's a smile that's lit up with mischief. 'Cold hands, warm heart,' she says, and I almost want to stop myself but I can't.

'Cold hands, cold heart,' I say, which is what Mammy always says, and I smile my special smile, just for her. I want to show her Dolly. I think Nancy would like Dolly, because Dolly is a lot like me and it seems that Nancy likes me. But I remember what Mammy has said, and so I keep quiet about Dolly. Instead, I put a hand out and rest it on Nancy's belly.

The night before, Nancy had come to me in the dining room, while I was helping Cook to clear away the dishes. 'Quick, Iris, come here,' she'd whispered, and grabbed me by the hand and dragged me into the hall, all the while Cook giving us an evil look.

'The baby's kicking again!' she'd exclaimed, and she'd taken my hand and placed it on her belly. At first, I felt nothing, the taut surface of her stomach pressed against my flat palm. And then I felt the beat: once, twice, three times, thumping like my heart does when I've run up from the lake. Nancy was beaming, and for the first time, I felt sad for one of the Ladies.

Now, it seems natural for me to place my hand there. She'd said she could be a big sister to me, and isn't this what sisters do? I hope Dolly would not be jealous. Nancy shifts slightly, so that she's lying flat on the floor, relaxed. She's looking at me from the sides of her eyes, and there's a glint there.

'Do you know how babies are made, Iris?' She asks it innocently enough, but I can see her mouth twisting up a bit at one side. I try to make myself blush, but I can't, so instead I look away.

'No, I don't,' I say, and all the while I'm trying not to show the smile that's building up inside. She's looking at me properly now, I can tell, even though I've made myself look down into my lap. She's probably thinking that why should I, with my funny eyes and teeth and my stringy white hair, know about babbies? I'd not be going down that road, for sure. It'd take a fair strong-hearted lad to fuck that one, Nancy's thinking, and the thought of it makes the giggle rise in my chest. It erupts through my nose and I try to pretend that it's because I'm shy. 'No, Miss Nancy,' I say. 'I don't know how babbies are made.'

She takes a deep breath. 'When a man and a woman love each other very, very much—' And she stops because I've snorted snot all over the top of my pinafore and she's looking proper affronted.

'I'm sorry…' I say, and I'm enjoying every minute of this. I resurrect my face into a temple of innocence, pulling my brows up, my eyelids disappearing upwards. 'Please would you start again, and tell me how babbies are made?'

She thinks for a moment, then her lips come into a smile.

'I think that can probably wait for now,' she says, but not unkindly. She settles herself up on her bum again, and picks up her magazine.

I might have had a sheltered life. I don't go to school and I don't have any friends – I've never even left Bank House – but I hear everything the Ladies say to each other when they come to stay. They don't think I'm listening – poor little Iris with her peculiar looks – but I sit in the background and they forget I'm there. I hear everything – all the details about how they came to be in their predicament, the men who got them in the family way, the friends who've found different solutions to the same problems: encounters with gin bottles and coat hangers down dark alleys. Yes, I may well be peculiar little Iris, whose looks make her the subject of derision or scorn or pity, but I hear things. As well as my books, the Ladies are where I get a lot of my education. And what an education it is! I soak it all up, like a sponge.

I go back to my dictionary. My favourite words so far: *Hamadryad: a wood nymph who dies in the tree in which she dwelt; Hamble: to make a dog useless for hunting by mutilating the balls of its feet; Harlot: a prostitute, or a woman of shallow virtue.*

It is a week until Christmas and Cook has started panicking. The snow has not stopped coming down and Clippety Pete still hasn't been able to get the car out of the driveway.

'There'll be no goose, of that I'm sure,' Cook says, her bosom heaving with the depth of her sigh, 'and we've no marzipan for the cake. It's like we're stuck with rationing all over again!'

Mammy manages to stay calm. 'We've a full pantry,' she says in a gracious voice that's still plump from the sherry she had with lunch, 'and Peter will go to the lake and see what's there. We could have a… cormorant or a couple of snipe, if there are no geese.'

'Oh, mistress, I don't know how to prepare a cormorant! Tell him to get us half a dozen mallards – that should keep us going a few days.'

Mammy raises her eyebrows, but she doesn't protest.

In the drawing room, the fire is roaring and Miss Eccles has transferred her attention to a red hat. She looks placid enough when I go in, the clicking of her knitting needles in competition with the spitting of the logs on the fire. Clippety Pete had to go and cut more logs yesterday – we're chomping through them like they're butter, he'd said – and they're still damp from sitting out in the snow. I stand there for a moment, until she looks up, and when she does, she doesn't look away immediately but gives me a little nod before turning back to her knitting. She's warming to me, I think. The hat is almost the same colour as her cheeks, and I wonder why she must sit so close to the fire.

Miss Riley didn't come down for breakfast this morning, and Mammy left her be, which I thought was odd at first, but then I remembered the barney the two of them had last night. I've never seen one of the Ladies get into a tizz with Mammy – they're usually meek as lambs when they meet Mammy with her big hands and her square jaw. But there's been something about Miss Riley since she arrived – those dark eyes with the shadows under them, and the hollow cheeks and her painfully thin shoulders. There's the way she was always staring out the window, until she took herself off to hide in her room every day.

She came down after dinner and asked Mammy if she could have a word. The pair of them went into Mammy's office, civil as you like, but I could tell there was trouble brewing, because Miss Riley had a face on her like a cat's arse, all puckered and scowling.

'When am I going to meet them?' was the first thing I heard her say, as I went to sit on the stairs.

'Meet who?' Mammy was keeping her voice calm then, talking quietly, and I could only just hear her.

'You know exactly who I mean. They're the reason I'm here.'

I put my hand over my mouth to stop myself chuckling. I'd never heard a Lady speak to Mammy like this, especially not one as quiet as Miss Riley.

'We all know why you're here, Peggy. You're here so that we can help you with your...' Here, Mammy's voice trailed off, and I wondered which word she would choose to use this time. Predicament? Situation? Circumstances? I'd heard them all before, of course. 'Troubles,' came Mammy's deep voice through the crack in the stairs, and I thought how that was not one of the words I'd heard before, but I liked it. It sounded like we were going to make her troubles go away.

'Indeed,' Miss Riley answered back straight away. 'I am here so that you can help me, and you have been paid handsomely in accordance with the execution of that responsibility.' I could imagine Mammy's eyes rolling at that. 'I have requested that I meet the people who are going to be adopting my baby, and I should be grateful if you would facilitate that on my behalf.'

I thought Mammy might be starting to lose her temper. It turns out I was right.

Dead Relatives

'Miss Riley. What you need to remember is that I have made no undertaking to introduce you to the adoptive parents of your child. There was never any mention of that throughout our business arrangements.'

'You have to be mad! What mother would hand her baby over to people she's never met before? It was implied in your advertisement that a meeting would be procured with the adoptive parents.'

I could hear the sneer in Mammy's voice when she spoke.

'If you choose to infer a falsehood from an advertisement in the *Evening Standard*, then that is your lookout, Miss Riley.' Mammy hissed out the 'Miss'. 'We have a strict policy that mothers do not meet the adoptive parents of their children and neither—' Here she paused a moment, as if deciding whether to carry on. 'Neither do we allow mothers any contact with their babies after the birth.'

There was a sharp intake of breath, which I knew would be Peggy, and, sure enough, the door to the office slammed open and out she strode, her bloated belly pushing forward absurdly on her tiny frame. She started to climb the stairs and halted with a start when she saw me. I hunkered myself into the wall and she stormed past me, using the banister to haul herself upwards. I considered telling her that Mammy said it was bad luck to pass someone on the stairs, but decided that it probably wasn't a good time.

Miss Riley still does not appear at lunchtime, and Nancy says she has heard her sobbing in her room. Everyone eats their trout in silence, apart from Veronica, who squeals when a stray bone gets stuck in her gum and then whimpers while she digs it out and puts it on the side of her plate. Daft cow. Mammy has a go at Cook for not filleting the fish properly, and Cook does a big old roll of her eyes when Mammy's not looking. I'll follow Cook into the kitchen later and grab the fish bones before she can get rid of them.

It's been a couple of days since I've been able to go to feed the dead tree. It hasn't snowed yet today, and what snow we've had, is hard and compacted and like ice under the feet, and the soles of my only pair of shoes have no grip anymore, so I slip and slide all over the place. I can picture the gaping hole, right at the bottom of the tree, half in the trunk and half in the roots. Hungry.

It was mostly covered in moss when I found it last summer. I'd been gathering flowers to make a posy for Dolly – she always liked the convolvulus that sprouted up in the flower beds next to the pond. Jenkins the gardener was cutting the grass with the old rotary mower, wheezing up and down the banks, stopping now and then to light a Woodbine and glare at me through the smoke. He'd only been with us for a couple of months, but he'd never taken to me, had Jenkins.

I'd just started getting my monthlies – the curse, Mammy called it, but I didn't see it like that. It meant that I was a woman, and that, one day, I might have a babby of my own. It also made it easier to track time, knowing when another month had passed, and so I'd worked out it had been at least a month since the last lot of Ladies had left.

It would have been easy to miss the hole in the dead tree, if it hadn't been for the forget-me-nots that were growing around the bottom of the trunk. I thought they would look nice with the convolvulus, so I grabbed a handful, and then my foot slipped and I half fell, and that's when I saw there was a hole under my foot. I pulled back the moss, ripping it off in handfuls, and there it was: a hole as dark and empty as a sinner's heart. I couldn't see inside it – it was far too dark – and the bright sunshine made it seem even darker. I picked up the moss I had removed, and, very carefully, arranged it so that the hole was hidden again. I took the posy I had picked for Dolly and went back to the house, to my bedroom. I didn't know then how important the dead tree was to become.

After lunch, I sit in the drawing room with Nancy and Veronica. Veronica's still complaining about the fish bone that got stuck in her jaw, rubbing occasionally at the sore spot, causing Nancy to roll her eyes at me. Veronica stops her whingeing in the end – she can't knit if she's always rubbing away at her face – and Nancy lies back on the sofa. I think she's dropped off, because she jumps with a start when the commotion starts in the hall. Miss Riley's standing there in her coat and gloves, her suitcase packed at her feet. She's even got her hat on, a fancy one that sits on top of her hair like a flowerpot. Her face is set like stone.

Cook comes in from the kitchen, rubbing her hands on her apron, and when she sees Miss Riley, she puts a hand up to her chest.

'Now, miss, what's all this about?' she says, in the voice she uses for pacifying Clippety Pete's bitch when it gets nervous.

'Fetch Mrs Sefton, please. I should like to leave.' Miss Riley's voice is clipped and sharp, and she sounds as though she's not going to stand for any nonsense.

'The mistress is having a lie down,' says Cook. 'If you'll just let me take your coat, you can go and wait in the drawing room with the other ladies, and then when Mistress is here I'm sure we can sort all this out.' There's a desperate sort of pleading in Cook's voice, and I know it's because she doesn't want to wake Mammy up from her afternoon nap. No-one has ever woken Mammy up from her nap.

'No, I refuse to wait. If Mrs Sefton is too drunk to come down, then ask that… man to drive me to the railway station.' Miss Riley is making no effort to keep her voice down, and it makes me giggle because no-one's ever dared call Mammy drunk before.

I'm aware of Nancy, and then Veronica, appearing behind me, drawn by the brouhaha in the hall. Then, there's a sudden silence, like a vacuum, and everyone turns to look up the stairs. Mammy is standing on the half-landing, her hair flat on one side, her skirt creased. She's fumbling to put her spectacles on and her face is thunder.

'Is there a problem, Miss Riley?' I'm surprised at how low and even Mammy's voice is, but then I see how her eyes are flashing. This is going to be good.

'I have no problem, Mrs Sefton.' Miss Riley is looking Mammy square in the eye, but there's a twitch in her left eyelid, a tic, and then I know this is all an act. She's scared. 'I should like to leave, that is all. I believe I have been…' Here she pauses, as if choosing her words carefully. 'I believe I have been invited here under false pretences.'

Mammy starts walking down the stairs, her hand clutching the banister carefully, her steps slow and deliberate. When she gets to the bottom she straightens her shoulders and gathers herself up to her full height. She is a full head taller than Miss Riley, and as broad as an ox. Miss Riley looks up at her, but her eyelid is still twitching. Then Mammy speaks.

'Very well. What are you waiting for? Off you go. Take yourself back to London and… whatever it is you do there.' Mammy's dismissal of Miss Riley has surprised her, I can tell. She stands there, looking up at Mammy, her mouth open. She was expecting a showdown.

'I—I—I should like a refund,' she manages to stutter out, and at this Mammy laughs, a great big hoarse, throaty chuckle, which echoes around the hall.

'Oh, I don't think so. We had an arrangement, you see, and I was quite clear that if you break the terms of the agreement, you forfeit your payment.' Mammy is speaking slowly and quietly, as though to an imbecilic child, and I put up a hand to cover the smile that I can feel growing on my face.

'I'll sue you. My father's a lawyer.' When Miss Riley says this, Mammy doesn't even pause.

'A lawyer, eh? Fancy. Does he know about the trouble you've got yourself into? Does he know why you're here?'

Miss Riley hesitates before answering. 'Of course he does. Why wouldn't he?'

'It's just that he seems to be under the impression that you're away at secretarial college. Whatever would give him that idea?'

A broad curtain of red climbs up Miss Riley's neck and paints her cheeks crimson.

'How—how do you know?' she asks, then realisation hits her. 'My letters! You've been reading my letters before you posted them!'

'I never even posted them, you jumped-up little bitch.' This is a lot, even by Mammy's standards, and I can feel Veronica flinch behind me.

'But—but...' Miss Riley's objection tails off, and she finally looks away from Mammy. There are tears springing in her eyes, and I almost feel sorry for her. Then I remember Mammy saying to Cook that it was her own fault she was here, if she'd been able to keep her legs shut she wouldn't be in the family way.

Miss Riley looks soft, deflated, and when she speaks her voice is flimsy and thin. 'Will you at least ask the man to drive me? I can't walk far in this...' Her voice tails off and I think she's going to say 'condition', or 'state', but instead she says, '...weather.' And she's right; there's a thick veil of snow coming down outside, and it looks denser than ever because the light out there is already starting to fail.

Mammy is not an especially kind person, but she's not cruel, either. She sends Cook out to the kitchen to fetch Clippety Pete, who takes an age to come hobbling through into the hall, and when he does he's wiping something off his chin. Mammy tells him to drop Miss Riley at the railway station, and he starts to protest that it's miles away, and he doesn't even know if he can get the car out and he's just started his cup of tea, but he soon dries up when he sees that Mammy's not taking any notice of him. In the end he grabs the suitcase roughly by the handle and yanks it out through the front door, grumbling all the time, and immediately he's covered in snow. Miss Riley seems to have gathered herself together. She wraps her scarf around her neck and pulls her hat down tighter over her hair, and without even looking at any of us, she follows him out into the weather. The door shuts behind them with a click.

Mammy marches towards the kitchen and Cook scuttles along after her. The three of us – me, Nancy and Veronica – go back and sit down in the drawing room. Nancy stays very quiet, and nestles herself into the corner of the sofa, chewing at her nails and gazing into space. Veronica picks up her knitting again, and for a while the clicking of the needles and the crackling of the fire are the only sounds that break the silence. Then there's a rustle as Nancy shuffles herself along the sofa so she's sitting right next to me. She's frowning.

'Is it always this way, Iris?' she whispers in my ear. She smells of rose water.

'I don't know what you mean,' I whisper back, even though I do. She heaves out a sigh. The knitting needles keep on tapping away.

'We don't get to meet the... the new parents? Is that right?' When I don't say anything she glances at Veronica and then back to me. 'Is that right?' she repeats. Even though she's still whispering, I've never heard her speak so sharply before and it startles me. She looks so concerned and vulnerable that I take pity on her. I put my hand on top of hers and give it a pat.

'It's fine,' I tell her. 'It's always like this. Mammy says that it's just upsetting for everyone – for the mothers and the new parents – if they meet. Better for all concerned to just be grateful for small mercies and get on with things, she says.'

She's silent for a minute or two, as if gathering her thoughts. Finally, she shrugs her shoulders and gives a little sniff. 'I suppose she's right. I'd just thought that I'd meet these people and then I would know what they were like, that I'd be able to imagine this baby growing up in a loving family. Something I couldn't give him or her. It just makes me sad, that's all.'

'It's for the best,' I tell her, and it feels as though I'm the grown-up and Nancy is the child.

Veronica looks up from her knitting. 'What are you two in cahoots about?' she asks.

Nancy looks at me and gives me a small, sad smile, with just the corners of her mouth. 'It's nothing,' she says. 'Iris was just filling me in on a few things, that's all.'

Veronica goes back to her knitting, and for a while nobody says anything. Nancy leans back and starts rubbing at her belly. She's gazing into the distance and she looks as though she's in another world. Then, it's as if she's suddenly come to her senses. Her arms thrust against the back of the sofa and she heaves herself up and asks Veronica if she can have a piece of wool. Veronica cuts her off a generous length which Nancy spools around her hand. She sits back down next to me and tells me to hold my hands out and spread out my fingers. She starts wrapping the wool around them, weaving it in and out.

'Have you ever done a cat's cradle?' she asks.

Mutely, I shake my head, and she carries on winding the wool. I'm glad that she seems happier now, less worried, and now it's nice again, after all the commotion earlier – the three of us, the fire blazing, sitting in silent camaraderie. After a few minutes, Nancy starts humming something, and Veronica joins in, and then Nancy starts singing – something about good vibrations. The two of them smile at each other.

'Do you like music, Iris?' Nancy asks, out of the blue. I think about the question.

'I'm not really... aware of music,' is the best answer I can come up with. Nancy looks up at me, her eyebrows raised.

'I mean, we don't really *have* music here – not even classical music, never mind all that modern stuff,' I manage. I'm conscious of Veronica peering at me over her knitting needles.

'And why's that, do you think?' Nancy's tongue is poking out as she winds the wool, the pink tip sticking out of the corner of her mouth.

'I suppose it's Mammy,' I say, before I can think about it. Nancy glances up at me. I take a deep breath. 'Mammy's always said that music is… a bad thing. That it encourages…' And here I pause, trying to remember Mammy's exact words. '…arrogance, slovenliness and depravity.'

Nancy snorts out a laugh, and Veronica joins in.

'Depravity! Can you imagine, Veronica?' Again, they share a smile, and ever so gently, I feel the hairs on my arms rise.

'Music's the thing I miss most about my old life,' Nancy announces. 'Before…' Here she uses the skein of wool to gesture at her belly. 'Music, and going out dancing, staying out all night if we wanted to. Drinking, laughing. God, I miss my friends.'

Now the hair on the back of my neck starts to bristle, and this makes me think of the pike up in its case on the landing, its fins twitching. Nancy carries on winding the wool around my fingers, looping it around itself, the contortions getting more and more complicated, my fingers caught tighter and tighter. I can feel the heat on my cheeks, hear the rush of blood in my ears.

And then I feel the word 'slattern' fall into my mouth. It sits there for a moment, hot and slippery, and before I can stop it, it jumps straight out again. I know it's Great Auntie Sarah saying it.

Nancy stops humming. Her face is white, and her mouth is open in a little 'o'. Veronica has stopped knitting and is looking at me, aghast.

'What did you say, Iris?'

I don't know how to reply, so I just look at my hands, wound all around with red wool. My skin feels as though it's been pickled – put into a pan with vinegar and sugar and boiled. It's tight and fidgety.

'Iris? I thought we were friends. That's not a nice thing to call someone.'

I realise that I have to say something. 'I'm sorry. I don't know why I said that. I know it's not a nice word, and I didn't mean it.'

'Is that what your mother calls me?' Nancy asks, ice in her voice.

I think of all the things I've heard Mammy call the Ladies, but shake my head. I panic.

'It was Dolly,' I say, then I remember that Nancy mustn't know about Dolly.

'Dolly?' she says. 'Who's Dolly?'

'Just a friend,' I whisper, so that Veronica can't hear. Nancy knows I don't go to school, and that I don't have any friends. Her face changes. She looks at me in her kindly way.

'Ah, I see. Don't you think, Iris, that you might be a little bit old to have an imaginary friend?'

I think about telling her that Dolly is real, that she's my best friend – not imaginary – and my sister as well, but then I can hear Mammy saying that I must never tell anyone about Dolly, so I just nod my head.

'Is Dolly jealous? Jealous of me, now that I'm your friend?' She's teasing me now, but I play along with her.

'She is, yes, but I've explained to her that you won't be here for much longer. As soon as the babby comes you'll go back to London and forget all about us.' If Nancy can hear the bitterness in my voice she doesn't mention it.

Nancy puts her hand on my knee. 'As soon as the baby is born I'll go back to London, yes, but I'll never forget about you, Iris.'

I wonder then if I should tell Nancy the truth about the babbies, so that she can make her own mind up, like Miss Riley did. I open my mouth, but then I think that she and Veronica can work it out for themselves, if they're such good friends, so I just smile and say nothing.

I have never told anyone that my earliest memory is of being born. It's not that I've been hiding it, it's just that I've never had anyone to tell, apart from Dolly, and I don't think she'd want to be reminded. At least, I think I can remember it. Perhaps I've made the memory up, given what I now know.

I remember a cocooned warmth, a red-black cardiac thump and the squeezing, the pushing and the tightness all around me followed by the surge through blood and goo and hair and the almighty plop into the light. The cold on my shoulders like a cloak, the intake of breath from Cook and panting sobs from Mammy.

Then the silence. That silence. Black silence, as though forever.

A sharp slap and the sudden rush of air in my lungs. Great, big, cool gushes of breath and more gasps and more sobbing. And then, being swaddled in tight, rough sheets and picked up and the light in my eyes, the light. And then Cook's voice, trembling.

'I am sorry, Mistress. It's another one like the last.'

III

It's barely light when I leave the house the next morning and close the door carefully behind me, making sure it's on the latch. I stand under the portico for a moment and breathe in the brittle, chilly air. It feels good in my lungs, as though it's cleansing me from within. The moon's still up in the sky, bright and luminous, and there are a few stars, twinkling away. The lake lies flat and barren. It stopped snowing not long after Miss Riley left, and the garden is starting to look grubby. The snow has begun to melt in patches, grass and gravel showing through here and there. The trees are naked again, and stand taller now that they're not weighed down by their blankets of snow. I start the trek to the dead tree, doing my best to stick to the places where the snow has disappeared, so I don't leave any footprints.

It came as a shock last night when I realised how long it had been since I'd visited the tree and taken it sustenance. Nancy has been a distraction from my duties, I think. I tried to sneak into the pantry when Cook wasn't looking, to see what was in the scraps bowl, but she chased me out. 'I've enough work to do before tomorrow without you getting under my feet,' she bellowed. Clippety Pete had managed to catch a goose at the lake (a Canada goose, I think – *Branta canadensis*) and had wrung its neck. It was laid out on the kitchen table and Cook was plucking it, ripping off handfuls of feathers that floated in the air and settled on the floor. There were speckles of blood covering its skin, and that's when I remembered about my monthly rags that were still in the basket in the bathroom, waiting for Cook to wash them. Mammy had once told me, when I was little and didn't want to eat an egg because it had a blood spot in it, that blood was full of iron, and iron was good for you. I decided I would leave the rags in the tree and that would be plenty of nourishment.

The rags are rolled up tight in the pocket of my coat. There's a bit of a smell, but not a dirty smell. It's rich and ripe. I go past the pond and the greenhouse, and I stop to pluck a sprig of holly from the bush, the berries red and bloody: a Christmas present for the dead tree.

I can barely make it out in the gloom, but when I get to it, it feels as though it's been waiting for me. There's a sense of urgency, a hunger. I take the rags out of my pocket and bend down. I put my hand into the hole, holding the rags and the holly, but then pull it back again. Something moved in there.

I, and I alone, know about the tiny bundle of bones that resides at the bottom of the hole in the dead tree. Only I know how I found it in the summer, when I saw a piece of sackcloth floating on the surface of the lake, just off the shore. I grabbed a stick and used it to pull the cloth towards me, and I am the only one who knows that when I pulled it, sodden and dripping, from the water, and opened it out, it revealed a tiny skull, no bigger than the palm of my hand, round and smooth and creamy white. A babby's skull. And a tiny ribcage, the bones curved and fragile, pluckable like the strings of a harp. There was nothing else of the babby left, and I thought of the pike, patrolling the bottom of the lake, their enormous teeth ready to bite and chew and destroy.

The shrew that must have made its nest in the dead tree scampers away into the undergrowth, a flash of grey in the dawn light. Nothing else moves. I lean in again and I drop the rags and the holly onto the sackcloth bundle. Even though I can't see it, I know it's there, covered by all the offerings of sustenance I've left for it over the months. Poor babby.

Since Miss Riley left, it is as though something has lifted in the house. Mammy seems happier – and why not; she's getting to keep the money and there's one less mouth to feed – and Cook seems to be getting in the Christmas spirit. By the time Christmas Eve comes around, there's an almost convivial spirit in the house. Even Clippety Pete has stopped glaring at me when he trudges through the house to Cook's parlour.

The smell coming from the kitchen is enough to cheer anyone up; Cook has been roasting the goose for hours, and peeling potatoes and parsnips and steaming the Christmas pudding. It'll be a real feast. Clippety Pete went out and cut a branch off one of the yew trees in the garden (*Taxus baccata*, according to H.R. Milner's *Coniferous Trees of the Northern Hemisphere*) and planted it in a pot like a Christmas tree. Nancy and I have hung paper chains on it, and Veronica has knitted a star from yellow wool which we pinned to the top. Even Mammy said how festive it looked.

It was Nancy's idea, to have a sing-song. 'Like they do in the East End pubs,' she'd said, and Mammy snorted at that, and I could feel her starting to bristle, her mood shifting, but she didn't say anything.

'Now, Iris, what are you going to sing for us?' asks Nancy, and I can feel everyone looking at me, their eyes burning into me, making my cheeks sting. Mammy's peering at me over the top of her spectacles.

'I—I—I don't know any songs,' I say, and it's true. Nancy and Veronica knew how Mammy felt about music, that we never sang in our house and that we had no wireless or even a gramophone player. The only time I'd heard Cook let out a tune was when Clippety Pete was battering away at her from behind in the pantry.

It's as though Nancy suddenly remembers what I told her and sees how fearful I've become, because she decides to rescue me.

'Let's sing some Christmas carols,' she says. 'I'll tell you what, how about "Away in a Manger"? Let's all sing it together.' And we do. Me and Nancy and Veronica, and after a while even Mammy starts singing, because even Mammy can't object to the singing of Christmas carols. By the time we get to the last verse, Cook and Clippety Pete have decided to come in from the kitchen and join in.

'Bless all the dear children in Thy tender care, and take us to Heaven to live with Thee there.'

*

It's not often that Clippety Pete and Cook share a table with us, even though they've lived with us forever. Cook's mammy was a cook here even before I was born (and she was called Cook as well), and Clippety Pete's father used to maintain the house before he died and Pete took over. It's like we're one big family, who have always lived in Bank House together. Mammy, though, says that servants should know their place, and not get above themselves, but she makes an exception on Christmas Day, and usually it's the four of us around the dining table.

This is the first time we've had Ladies to stay at Christmas, and the table's not really big enough for all of us. Mammy sits at the head of the table, in the oak settle chair I think of as a throne; Mammy is nothing if not majestic. I sit opposite her, and Clippety Pete is on my left. He looks uncomfortable in his tweed jacket, and keeps fidgeting in his chair. There is a place set for Cook opposite him, where she'll sit when she's finished clattering about in the kitchen. The Ladies are expected to sit on either side of Mammy, and Veronica is already there on Mammy's left. She's put her knitting needles away for once, and doesn't seem to know what to do with her fingers – she keeps twisting them around themselves. In the end Mammy slaps her hands and Veronica mutters a 'sorry' and sits on them to keep them still. Cook puts her head around the kitchen door.

'Is she still not here, then?' she asks.

We're still waiting for Nancy. We have been ever since Mammy rang the dinner bell ten minutes ago.

'Veronica, do go and see where she's got to,' Mammy says, irritably, but then, as Veronica begins the long process of hauling herself to her feet, Mammy changes her mind and tells me to go. And that is when Nancy appears in the doorway. She's wearing a dress I haven't seen before – a dark pink number that finishes a good few inches above the knee. It has a deep-cut neckline that shows a lot of her titties, and the fabric stretches snugly across her swollen belly. The sleeves are full, elbow-length, and are embroidered with blue and green flowers. With her hair flowing over her shoulders, she looks like a goddess. Everyone has stopped talking and is looking at her, and she blushes slightly as she walks to the table. She catches a heel on the carpet, and her hand goes out to steady herself against the back of the chair, and that's when I see her shoes – silver, with pointed toes and little bows at the front.

Mammy's face is thunder. Cook looks as though she's going to be sick. Clippety Pete is staring as though he's never seen titties before, but, to be fair, he's probably only ever seen Cook's great big flabby giblets.

'You should have started without me,' Nancy says, heaving herself into her chair. 'I wouldn't want it to get cold.'

Mammy harumphs. 'You'll be the one getting cold, dressed like that,' she says. 'You'll catch your death if you're not careful.'

'Thought I'd make a bit of an effort, that's all,' Nancy says airily, and settles herself into her chair. I can feel my dead relatives goading me, telling me to say something, and in my head I beg them to leave me alone.

For a while, no-one says anything. Clippety Pete and Veronica both continue to fidget, and Mammy glares at everyone and no-one in particular. Nancy gives me a nod and I nod back. And then Cook nudges open the door from the kitchen with her great big arse and slams a tray down in the middle of the table. The flesh of the goose is crisped and golden, and it sits on a sheen of gleaming fat. Everyone – even Mammy – draws in a breath. Cook's eyes are shining. I think of the goose laid out on the kitchen table, speckled with its own blood and surrounded by a pile of feathers. Now the head has been cut off at the base of the neck, the skin tucked in and puckered. The feet have been cut off and left in stumps. It looks delicious.

Cook goes back to the kitchen, and she returns with a plate piled high with golden roast potatoes, and another with vegetables – parsnips, cabbage, swede and sprouts. Another trip to the kitchen brings gravy and bread sauce. Mammy nods at Cook, and, although she says nothing, I can tell that she approves. Then she aims another nod at the sherry bottle on the sideboard, and I know that is the signal for Cook to fill three glasses – one for Mammy and one each for Cook and Clippety Pete. A rare treat.

Mammy starts to carve, and the smell of roasted meat becomes even more enticing. She lays slices of goose on plates and these are passed round by Cook. When I get mine, I try to pinch a piece off my plate and stuff it in my mouth, but Mammy sees and glares at me. The waiting is killing me.

'Now then,' Mammy says when everyone has a plate in front of them. 'Please everyone help yourselves to vegetables, and let's be grateful to Cook for this wonderful feast.' Everyone claps and Cook beams and blushes, and Clippety Pete clears his throat.

'And Peter,' says Mammy with a trace of irritation in her voice. 'Thank you to Peter as well for procuring this magnificent bird.' Pete nods and looks at the table.

Dead Relatives

My plate is piled high with food and I'm waiting for Mammy to say that we can start, when I notice that she is looking intently at Veronica on her left. Veronica is leaning back in her chair, her hands clasped over her stomach. She's making a face like she's sucking on a lemon, and then she starts huffing and puffing. Mammy rolls her eyes and looks at Cook.

'It's starting,' she states flatly, and Cook looks thoroughly annoyed. Pete starts shovelling food into his mouth, but Nancy and I are watching in silence.

'After all this,' says Cook, sounding like she might cry. 'After all this trouble I've gone to and she starts now. She's got another month to go, and all.'

Mammy shrugs and knocks back her glass of sherry.

In the end they decide that the contractions are far enough apart for Veronica to be put on the sofa in the drawing room while we finish our lunch. Cook gives her a hot water bottle for her belly and a hard glare, and then we sit back down at the table. The festive spirit has gone, though. Clippety Pete has finished his food and is sitting back in his chair. Cook looks angry, munching away in silence. Mammy just carries on chewing, like she's got a job to do and no-one's going to stop her. Only Nancy stops eating, and she keeps glancing nervously at the door that leads through to the hallway, off which sits the drawing room and Veronica.

The commotion starts soon after I make a start on 'M' in the dictionary. Nancy and I are in our den on the landing, surrounded by the stuffed birds and fish and with my dead relatives all gathered round. In everyone there is an air of anticipation, and each of my ancestors has an added gleam in their eyes. It's always like this, when the Ladies go into labour, as though there will shortly be something to celebrate. Only Auntie Maude looks concerned, as she does each time. Mammy told me she died in childbirth, so I think this brings it all back to her.

Madder: a herbaceous plant whose root produces a red dye; Magic: the art of producing marvellous results by compelling the aid of spirits; Malady: illness, disease, whether of the body or the mind. A faulty condition.

Nancy has got changed out of her pretty dress and has helped herself to Veronica's abandoned knitting. She has taken it upon herself to finish it. The trouble is, she's not as good a knitter as Veronica, and she keeps tutting as she drops stitches. I don't think Veronica will be pleased with the help Nancy is giving her, but Nancy says she needs something to take her mind off things. That's when the screaming starts.

It's a bloody awful sound, and I say that as someone who has witnessed this sort of thing for as long as I can remember. We can hear Veronica screeching, plain as day, from her room all the way up in the attic. Nancy stops knitting, and looks up at the ceiling, as though she can see right through the plaster and the beams and the floorboards and the rug, all the way through the iron bed and the lumpy mattress and the sheets to where Veronica will be lying, squeezing out her baby. There's more screaming, and then silence for an agonisingly long stretch of time, and then the plaintive wail of a newborn. Nancy's eyes are huge in the gloom of the landing. Then Cook comes dashing down from the attic. She doesn't see us, nestled into our corner. She runs all the way downstairs, and I know that she'll be fetching Clippety Pete. Sure enough, a minute later (*Malaise: uneasiness, discomfort; a feeling of debility or impending sickness*) she comes stomping back up again, Pete hobbling after her. In his hand, swinging with the momentum of climbing the stairs, is a sack.

When I am a bit older, I will learn how to deliver babbies. Mammy will teach me, as Granny Violet taught her. We have a great tradition of midwifery in this family, Mammy is fond of telling me, and a great tradition of helping the Ladies. I've never really questioned why we – because I feel involved in this as well – do what we do. It's something that has always happened at Bank House: more than two hundred years of delivering babbies. True, it's only a matter of time before the new law comes in which will let the Ladies get rid of their babbies, and we'll have to find another way of making a living. The times, as one of the Ladies from last summer kept singing, they are a-changing.

Nancy's eyes are black holes in the gloom of the landing, her face a grey mask. It's almost dark this late in the afternoon, and I can't make out her expression when she asks, 'What is the sack for, Iris?' Her voice has a tremor in it, a rattle like the dead tree has when the wind picks up and shakes its naked branches.

I think of the babby I found, its bones clustered in the sackcloth, the smooth swell of the cranium, the ribcage, fragile as an eggshell. I don't know what to say to her, so I pick up the dictionary and the first word my eyes land on is *Malediction: cursing, a calling down of evil, a curse.*

'Tell me, Iris.' The tremor has gone from Nancy's voice, and now she is whispering, urgently, insistently. 'What is the sack for?'

Malefactor: an evil-doer, a criminal; Malfeasance: evil-doing, wrong-doing, an illegal deed. Deceit.

I clear my throat. 'It's for the bedding. It gets covered in blood, you see, when the babby's born. They want to get it down to the scullery as quick as they can, before the sheets stain.' I look up at her, even though her face is just a veil in the darkness. 'Blood can be terribly hard to get out of linen.'

After a couple of days' recuperation, Clippety Pete drives Veronica to the railway station. She and Nancy say goodbye in the hall, and hug each other, even though Nancy's belly puts a good distance between them. Veronica is pale and walks awkwardly, but she seems relieved to be going home. They promise to get in touch when Nancy's back in London, saying they'll meet up and have a night out.

'I can't remember what a night out is like!' says Nancy, patting her belly. 'We'll go dancing and have a few drinks and put the world to rights.' Veronica agrees, and the two of them swap addresses. She has not, as far as I am aware, mentioned her babby once, and I think after the ruckus with Peggy asking to meet the new parents, Veronica must have decided it's not worth incurring the wrath of Mammy.

After they have left, Nancy and I sit in the drawing room. There's something in the air, a heaviness that is waiting to be broken. Nancy is sitting in Veronica's chair, next to the fire, and is leaning back, her belly thrust out in front of her. She's stroking it, protective. Then she clears her throat.

'Do you think I'm doing the right thing, Iris?' She's not looking at me; she's staring into the fire, and the flames are reflected in her eyes, leaping and flickering.

'What do you mean?' I know what she means alright, but I don't know the answer just yet.

'About the baby. Perhaps I should keep it. It wouldn't be so hard. I'd take it back to London, get my own flat.'

'What about money?' I ask, because I know she's lost her job and doesn't get on with her parents, and in all this time together, she's never once mentioned the babby's father. She grimaces and gives a little shrug.

'I'll manage somehow. I'll find a job, and I've got friends who could look after the baby while I'm at work. And I've got some savings, and babies don't need to cost much and...' Her voice tails off, and there's another light in her eyes now, brighter than the reflected flames. Infinitesimally, her chin juts out, and her hand is smoothing, soothing her belly. Without her saying anything, I know she has made a decision.

There is no chaos or commotion the next day when, after eating a hearty breakfast of porridge and eggs on toast, Nancy asks Mammy for a word in her office under the stairs. From my seat on the fifth stair, I can hear Nancy explain that she has changed her mind and is going back to London. She will keep her babby and see if the father will have anything to do with it, financially. Mammy starts to complain, but Nancy interrupts her to tell her that she can keep the money she has been paid, that Nancy realises a deal is a deal. Mammy mutters something, but she's speaking so quietly I can't hear, and then Nancy comes out and shuts the door behind her very calmly. She walks past me up the stairs, and gives me a little smile, and I think she's not going to say anything, but then she turns back and says, 'Remember, Iris, that it's bad luck to pass someone on the stairs.' And then she's gone.

She appears half an hour later with her suitcase, and her coat is draped over her arm. Mammy has already told Clippety Pete that he has to drive Nancy to the railway station, and he's standing in the hall, his tweed jacket pulled sullenly over an old jumper. Mammy and Cook are in the kitchen. They don't do goodbyes.

There's something eating away at my heart. I've never felt like this before, and I don't know what it is. Is it sadness? Is it jealousy that soon Nancy and Veronica will be in London, not out dancing and having a good time, like they expected, but cooing over Nancy's babby together? She's my first friend, my only real friend, unless you count Dolly. It occurs to me that I hadn't considered losing her. I somehow thought she would stay here forever. My chest is tight and it's all I can do to look Nancy in the eye when she leans down and strokes my cheek.

'Take care, Iris,' she says in a quiet voice. 'It has been lovely knowing you, and I shall miss you dreadfully.'

It's Little Vera who answers, and with a word I thought an eight-year-old wouldn't know. The word sits in my mouth, heavy and gritty like a peach stone, and I fight it because I don't want to say it – I don't want my friendship with Nancy to end like this – but I'm not strong enough, and it comes hurtling out.

'Bitch!' I shout, even though I don't want to. And then I can feel Vera pushing me further, but calmer now, and in a whisper I say, 'Fucking bitch.'

Before I turn and run up the stairs, I see the shock on Clippety Pete's face, his furry eyebrows shooting up almost to meet his quiff, and then Nancy. Nancy's face has twisted into a mask of upset and revulsion, and something that I think might be fear. I don't wait to hear what she says. I'm up those stairs lickety split, all eighteen of them to the half-landing, and I grab the newel post and swing myself round and I'm up the next six to the top. I ignore Nanna Charlotte and Auntie Maude. I run straight past Great Auntie Sarah and Granny Violet and I know they'll be looking with eyebrows raised. I get to Little Vera and she's looking at me and she's smirking, a sickening curl on her lip that is the last straw. I pull back my arm and then I slam my fist into her smug, satisfied face. The glass cracks in a spiderweb of lines, and then falls onto the carpet in a delicate clatter. The pike in its glass case snarls.

That's when it occurs to me what I have to do.

Mammy was quiet at dinner. She didn't mention Nancy or what I had said to her. I think that Clippety Pete must have kept that particular nugget of information to himself. I'm not hungry, and I push the fried eggs and bubble and squeak around my plate. The fat smears onto the porcelain, greasy like the vernix on a newborn babby. In the end, Mammy gets annoyed and tells me to leave the food and go to my room.

Dolly is sitting where I left her on my pillow. Her christening gown is grubby, the lace and silk yellowed with age. There is no photograph of Dolly on the landing wall. There was no time to take one before she died. She was three days old and they did not know that she was going to die. They should have guessed, I thought. They should have been able to tell by the state she was in when she came out of Mammy: her face squashed, her nose tiny and flat, the nostrils huge black holes. Her mouth is open in a silent cry, and I wonder if she was like this when she died, hungry and crying for milk that Mammy couldn't give her because her mouth was the wrong shape to suckle.

Dolores Rose Sefton. My sister. Sefton babbies are always girls – there hasn't been a boy born to a Sefton in this house for over two hundred years. She has no ears, only holes in the sides of her head, and even before Clippety Pete did his best with her, her skin might have been this shade of yellow, like my morning piss. There are stitches running up her stomach, the skin puckered around the thread where Pete would have stitched her up. He'd have emptied her insides out and replaced them with sawdust after pickling her skin in alum and borax. No photographs exist, just this desiccated, dried-out husk that was, for three days, my big sister, before I was even born. And now my best friend.

I gather Dolly in my arms and tiptoe down the corridor to the landing. My dead relatives look on, curious, but I don't let them slow me down. In the hall, I can hear Mammy and Cook talking in the dining room. I slip out of the front door, remembering to lift it on its hinges so that it doesn't creak. The cold leaps into my mouth and makes my teeth sting. I hold

Dead Relatives

Dolly closer and my skin is alive with goose pimples under my pinafore. There is a high, full moon, and a dusting of snow on everything glitters and shines, luminous in the dark.

The gravel crunches under my feet and I look around for Clippety Pete. He's not around, but his dog is. She's tied up outside the stable, and when she sees me, she starts whining. I have to walk past her, in order to get to the dead tree, and feel a tug of pity for her being out here in the bitter cold, but I have a job to do and keep on walking. The pond is a mirror for the stars, and when I get to the greenhouse, some of the remaining panes reflect the sky, the peculiar angles of the glass in their frames rendering a dozen moons, blurred. I follow the curve of the path, careful not to lose my step or slip in the greasy snow. And then I am standing in front of the dead tree.

It looks different, yet also the same. The branches retain their jagged angles, jutting sharply into the sky, the moon balanced on the axis where two branches join. The trunk shows papery grey in the brittle light, even though I know that in daytime it looks black and dead. It is as though the tree knows that I have come to feed it, to give it real sustenance this time, and is waiting, impatient and hungry.

Dolly's gown wraps around her like a shroud. I hold her in one hand, and with the other I brace myself against the tree's trunk. It feels warmer than it should, as though my presence has already started to restore life to it. I lean forward, and very carefully, ever so gently, kiss Dolly's flattened forehead. Then I place her in the hole in the tree. I don't bother to cover her up or hide her – I know the tree will take care of that. She will be a friend for the babby in there; everyone needs a friend. I straighten up and silently say goodbye.

When I turn around, the lake is flat and black and smooth. I think of all the bones in there: two centuries' worth of tiny babbies put there by my dead relatives. The end of an era. Close to shore there is a faint ripple which puckers the surface briefly and then disappears. The tears feel icy when they slide down my cheeks.

Jutland

There are birds gliding alongside the ferry as it churns its way across the North Sea. She doesn't know what they are, gulls of some sort probably, but she is struck by how graceful they are, streamlined for perfect flight. She has read somewhere that birds' bones are hollow. They are filled with air to make them lighter so that they can fly and that is what sets them apart from other creatures. It also makes their bones more fragile and susceptible to damage. You can't have it all, she thinks.

Eric stands, both hands on the glass, his face pushed right up, almost touching. He's like a child, and she knows that he's trying not to flinch as the waves crash against the ferry and splash up against the glass. To his right stands Isaac, hands by his sides, his little body swaying gently with the rocking of the boat. She can see that he has anchored himself to the deck using the weight of his body and sheer willpower, his feet planted wide apart just like Eric has shown him. That's how she feels herself most days now, as if she needs to root herself into the ground.

The baby lies in her lap, flat out along her thighs, its head resting against her knees. Its fleshy hands are furled and its eyes are squeezed shut, as though the light is too much for its tiny brain to bear. The rocking of the ferry has soothed it and sent it to sleep.

Through the foam-licked glass she can make out the shape of the headland. She cranes her neck to see past Eric, to see the craggy rocks that protrude from the sea, the water angry around them. She's still holding the guidebook, the one she's been reading for the entire journey from Gothenburg. That's not right: she's been looking at it, her eyes tracking the words, left to right, then down and left to right again, turning the page and then starting again, and in the whole of the last four hours she remembers nothing of what she has read. She doesn't know how; it's not as though she's been distracted by other things. The baby's been mostly asleep, drained of energy by being awake for most of the previous night. She's even managed to ignore the couple who sit opposite her, their bodies turned inwards in a conspiracy of intimacy, laughing, their voices low. Newly-weds, she thinks.

A loud scraping noise and the boat judders. The baby wakes and mewls, thrusting its bunched fist into its mouth, its eyes still squeezed tight. The headland is much nearer now, poised above them like a primal beast. The cliffs loom dark and unforgiving, grey and pocked with ledges that have been carved out by the sea or the wind, where seabirds roost. The birds here are graceless, flapping out into the churning air before they are flummoxed by the currents, tossed and battered and fluttering like confetti, until they catch a drift of warm air and start to glide. Like a child, she thinks, learning to walk.

Jutland

The decision to move to Jutland had been easy. Eric's obsession with the Skagen painters – Ancher, Krøyer, Johansen – had fuelled his insistence that they needed to get away so he could concentrate on his art. His last exhibition had been deemed a great success, with enthusiastic reviews appearing in the national as well as the local press. This was his time, he'd said, his time to shine. Ana was still on maternity leave, and her repeated attempts to revive the novel were thwarted. Baby brain, they'd called it. Cotton-wool between your ears, the health visitor had said. It'll clear. But for now just enjoy being with your children.

The baby's cries grow louder and more insistent as she straps it into the sling. She thinks that it is probably hungry, that it hasn't been fed since they got on the ferry, and as if her own body has betrayed her, and is working in collusion with this tiny creature, she feels the warm dampness spread across her sweatshirt. Fuck. It's too late to do anything about it now; the ferry has docked and people are standing up, gathering their belongings and preparing to disembark. Eric has turned from the window and is looking at her, and she thinks he might be trying to ask her something. She holds his eye and the baby is still squawking.

And then she sees Isaac looking up at her, silent, his pale face as impossible to read as ever. His refusal to talk has become both a concern and an irritant, but his father is enthusiastic that a change of scenery may encourage their son to end his silence.

Eric had shown her pictures of the cottage on the internet. Squat and long, like the one they'd stayed at in Norway before they had the children. They had rented the house for a week then, looking forward to escaping from the city and 'living with nature', Eric had joked. It had been horrible, but they hadn't cared. They'd sat in front of a fire that billowed smoke into the room, snuggled naked under a blanket, sipping aquavit and talking about what the future held, about Eric's imminent graduation from art college. The warm reception given to her first novel had still been tangible.

That was when the dreams had started, or moments of semi-consciousness in that grey hinterland between sleep and waking. It would be dawn, and fully formed sentences would alight in her mind, the words fitted together by an unseen craftsman, adept at manipulating the syllables and words into perfect rhythms. They would disappear before she could grab her notebook, and even the act of rousing herself to locate it on the nightstand would chase them away, but it was enough to send her into the day with the knowledge that she could, and she would, write.

She hasn't experienced this liberty for the last couple of months, not since the baby was born, those early-morning moments of lucidity lost to a wearily predictable fog of lost sleep, nappies and feeding.

They drive out of the belly of the ferry and into the sunlight and the port is nothing like she'd expected. It is a place of steel and tarmac, preposterous cranes that stand guard over the horizon, and scuttling ants in hi-vis jackets. Not the picturesque fishing village she'd had in mind. They drive for half an hour north, racing the sun as it threatens to set, and when they arrive at their destination, she sees that it is, after all, what she was hoping for. A tiny village, it consists of little more than a long terrace of white-painted houses that hugs the shoreline in a close caress, with nothing but a narrow road and a low stone wall to keep the sea at bay. How high does the tide rise, she wonders.

At the end of the row of houses there's a church, low and white-rendered, its red-tiled roof a welcome splash of colour against the onset of dusk. The church is separated from the lane by a picket fence, and she twists in her seat as they drive past, feeling inexplicably drawn to the little building. She knows that she will visit.

They drive for another five minutes, through the village and out the other side. The sat-nav has quit but Eric seems to know where they are going. Eventually he grunts, a sign she interprets as meaning that they are close, and she sees the house, high up on the hill, its long and low frontage thrown into deep shadow by the sun that sets behind it. The car meanders up the track towards it, and the house disappears now and then, hidden behind gorse hedges, before reappearing, its back towards the steep bank that rears up behind. She thinks of it as a solid house, an unyielding house.

Finally, they park. She extricates the baby from the car seat and it starts to bawl again, a screech that causes her skin to prickle. She straps it into the sling, its little fingers furling and unfurling all the time. Eric has picked up Isaac, who looks around sleepily, and he leads the way up the short path to the front door. She walks behind him, stepping carefully over the pebbles that form the pathway. The wind is strong at her back, not just pushing her along, but pushing down on her shoulders. It feels heavy, and it adds to the weight of the baby. She thinks that if she is blown over her brain will have to make a split-second decision about whether to put her hands out to break her fall and protect herself, or keep her arms around the baby and stop it from being damaged. She turns her back on the house and tastes salt on her lips.

From here, she looks down towards the sea, which is furrowed and rough. The tide is out, and on the shore stands a single figure: a child, a boy, she thinks, and she looks around for a parent, or an older sibling. There is an outcrop of rocks to the right, blackened against the silvery water, and she expects at any moment to see a figure come striding around it, berating the child for wandering off, and she wonders if she would be able to hear a voice from this distance, whether the wind would carry it this far. She turns back to the child to check its progress. There is no-one there; the vast expanse of beach is empty. She turns back to the house.

Eric has let himself in, and she steps through the doorway after him, the baby shrieking now. She finds herself in a kitchen, long and low like the house itself, and she is shocked by how cold it is, even colder than outside. Under the glare of an overhead strip light, she spots a wicker chair in one corner, and perches on the edge. She unstraps the sling and lays the baby in her lap. It is screaming now, red cheeks inflated in indignation, and she feels a prickle of guilt. That's good.

She unhooks the clasp on her sodden bra and offers her breast to the infant. It takes a moment to find her nipple, its head lolling back and forth. Then it pinpoints the scent of her milk and homes in, latching on, its tiny size belying its strength. She feels the dampness of its bottom against the palm of her hand, and at the same time she catches the smell of shit.

Jutland

'So what do you think?' Eric's voice is dry and strained, and Ana realises that they have barely spoken since they left Gothenburg that morning. He is addressing Isaac, not her, and her son replies in the only way he can or will: two thumbs up and a half-smile.

'And Ana. What about you?'

She shifts the baby on her lap, trying to get comfortable, but feeling the familiar ache in her lower back. She hears the brusqueness that will be evident in her voice even before she speaks. 'How would I know? And why would I have an opinion? I'm just a milking machine, aren't I?' Instantly, she regrets her outburst. And then she doesn't.

Morning sunlight intrudes through the gap between the curtains. Eric lies next to her, snoring gently in that way that used to be endearing. In this early, insipid light, his straw-coloured hair appears grey, even at the sides where in normal light it would sprout ginger.

She hears the baby's soft breaths from where it lies in the Moses basket on her side of the bed, and she rolls over. The minute chest rises and falls, the fabric of its tiny sleeping bag lifting and then dropping a fraction of a centimetre each time.

She eases herself from the tangle of sheets, and places her feet carefully on the cold stone floor. Her head is still thick with sleep, and with lost sleep. She was up with the baby on three occasions in the night, each time quick to jump from the bed before its cries woke Eric. She thinks that her body is programmed to react to the baby's sounds. Each morning she searches the peripheries of her memory for traces of words, of sentences that may have visited her in the night while she slept, a sign that she is still a writer. Nothing. Baby machine.

In the bathroom she squats and urinates. She watches the tap over the bath drip into the stagnant water that has gathered at the bottom, six inches of grey, and she wonders how long it has been accumulating. There must be a blockage somewhere; she will ask Eric to investigate. She stands to wash her hands at the basin, and through the clear glass of the little window she can see the glitter of the sea, and the promise of a new day where water and air might meet. It is the light that has brought them here. That cold, lucid light that trips in over the North Sea, bringing with it the threat of ice and nightmares. It merges the sea and sky; the horizon holds little sway here.

She showers briskly in the tiny cubicle, and the mildewed shower curtain clings cold against her back.

She heads for the kitchen to make coffee, and on her way she passes their bedroom door, and pauses to listen for sounds of the baby snuffling itself awake. Satisfied that there are none, she continues down the long corridor at the back of the house. She passes the second bedroom, where she knows Isaac will be asleep. She walks past the living room, filled with the boxes that still need to be unpacked. This will become Eric's studio, and even now his canvases take up most of the space. She has brought very little: some clothes and books, and her notebooks and laptop, for what they're worth.

She walks past the dining room, where they had sat last night after dinner, she and Eric alone in their own silences. It is as though Isaac's refusal to talk has infected them both, as if there is now no need for them to communicate, except on the most basic of levels. Cocooned in this silence, last night she had found herself reading again, properly reading, gorging herself on the words and revelling in their harmonies. A positive sign: if she is receptive to the words of others, she will somehow find her own voice again.

Finally, she arrives at the kitchen, and here she stands at the sink and fills the kettle and looks out into the morning.

She places the baby in the pram and tucks the blankets around it. Isaac has dressed himself, ever compliant, and stands, squinting up at her on the doorstep. There is a brisk wind and it lifts the curls that escape from his hat, but the spring sun is warm and welcome. They set off, their destination the village. Eric needs time and space to paint.

They have rounded the headland when she sees the boy again. He is standing on the beach, fifty metres from where she has stopped. He is silhouetted against the dazzling water, and she can't tell if he is facing them or if his back is turned and he is gazing out over the ocean. He stands very still, his arms hanging outwards slightly from his body. She thinks he is a bit taller than Isaac; he is certainly broader, the width of his shoulders suggesting a boy caught between infancy and childhood. She wonders whether to approach him, but can see no path down the steep slope to the beach. Perhaps she should shout out to him, ask where his parents are or whether he needs help. She is bracing herself to call out into the wind when the baby whimpers, and she bends to tuck the blanket in around it. When she looks up the boy has gone.

They make the descent to the village, and when the road levels off she steers the pram along the shoreline to where the little church stands alone in its patch of graveyard. With the benefit of the late-morning light she can see that although the grass is trimmed and there are neat vases of flowers placed here and there, the graves are jammed up hard against one another, and a sudden thought occurs to her: this is a place that likes to keep its dead close.

She does not go into the churchyard, but stands at the wooden gate and her eyes are drawn up, up to the cross that projects from the roof. Then her eyes move down, scanning the façade of the little church, its white wall brilliant in the sunlight. It makes her squint.

The wind whips a strand of hair across her mouth, and she raises a hand to remove it. She looks around for Isaac and sees that he has wandered along the lane and is crouching, attending to something that sticks up from the grass, close to the lane side of the picket fence. She walks towards him, leaving the baby sleeping in the pram. Isaac is holding a stone and is using it to scratch something onto a rock protruding from the ground. She steps closer and sees that it is a gravestone, smaller than usual, but undeniably just that, with its lichened, slab-like surface. It is only half a metre high, and it sticks up at a slight angle, like a milk tooth waiting to come free. Isaac has picked up a sharp stone and has scratched away some of the moss, has carved an 'I' and part of an 's'. She grabs him by the wrist and flings the stone away. Before she can even begin to admonish him, he starts bawling, and then she hears the baby screaming.

The man standing over the pram is shorter than Eric, but lean and muscular. When he turns to her, she sees that he has a beard which grows down his neck and disappears into his sweater. Not tidy enough for a hipster, she thinks. A fisherman perhaps. His eyes are narrowed against the sun.

'Your baby?' he says, and she nods.

'And your boy?' he asks. She turns to where Isaac is standing, snivelling and rubbing his nose. She nods again.

'You're new in the village?' he asks, and she is surprised at how easily her schoolgirl Danish comes back to her.

'Yes. New,' she says. 'We're renting the cottage up on the hill. Past the headland. The final house in the village. Living there six months.'

The man's eyes flicker to the space behind her, to where the little headstone sits, tight up against the fence that separates the lane from the graveyard. He doesn't say anything, but moves his hand in front of his face in a rapid motion, and Ana thinks that perhaps he is making the sign of the cross. It is a strong hand, she thinks, leathery and tanned, a hand that is used to outdoor labour. From the back pocket of his jeans he pulls a packet of tobacco and starts to roll a cigarette.

'And what does your husband do?'

Ana almost laughs in his face. Her husband? Was this still to be about him? 'I'm a writer and my husband is a painter,' she says.

'Came for the light, did he, like all the rest? What does he paint?'

She sees herself laughing. On top of a cliff, perhaps. The wind is pulling her hair backwards behind her face. She is free and joyful and has no encumbrances.

'He paints shit. He paints like shit. He is shit. But me? I'm a writer. Would you like to hear about that? About the awards I have won and the reviews in the broadsheets?' If she had actually said those words, Ana knows that she would be embarrassed. Instead she mutters something about impressionism and bends to tuck the blanket in around the baby.

'Tell him to come round for a beer,' the man says. 'I'm in the house at the far end.'

'Tell him yourself,' she says and catches the flicker in his eye. It is a look she knows. 'Come and visit,' she says. 'Come and visit and tell him yourself.'

The man puts the cigarette in his mouth and lights it, the flame of the Zippo working hard against the wind. When he looks up, his eyes dart briefly behind her, to the tiny headstone that stands on the verge of the lane, just outside the churchyard.

'Just tell him, yeah?'

There is only one way back from the village, and again they traverse the shoreline, the freshly laid tarmac an anachronism against the ancient light reflected by the sea. The baby is hungry again, and is crying, and so is Isaac. His hunger has been temporarily stemmed with a lolly from her bag, but there is something else about him, a mild form of distress that he can't or won't enunciate and that she is bored of trying to guess at. It is uphill all the way, and she feels her calves complaining as they reach the promontory.

But once there, she stops, stands up straight and breathes in the hard, blue air. She finds herself looking for the boy on the beach. He is not there. When she looks down, checking that the baby is still fully covered against the cold, she catches a glimpse of a gorse bush surrounded by entrails of twigs and straw. She steps closer. She sees a nest. Inside are eggs, four blue eggs, speckled with brown. She knows that if she were to pick one up and rub it with her thumb, it would feel chalky – rough and satisfactory.

She begins to straighten, and then she sees the gull. It is only a couple of feet in front of her and she doesn't know how she missed it. It is a large bird, white with a black head and black wings. It is unbothered by her. She walks closer, hunkering down, making herself smaller as she approaches. It doesn't flinch. It is busy. It is eating a chick, a nub of flesh and sodden grey down that it holds beneath the claws of one foot while its bright orange beak inspects the carcass.

Her first instinct is to flap her hands and shout and get that bloody bird away from the chick, but something in her shifts. She feels her insides loosen. She leaves the gull to its feast. She leaves nature to do what nature does and she walks back to the house. Isaac and the baby are silent all the way.

She is reading in the dining room when the baby wakes and starts to bawl. It is very late, and Eric is eking out the last of the daylight as he paints in his studio. She walks down the long corridor to the bedroom, and without turning on the light, she picks up the baby. Her presence seems to soothe it, and it quietens and regards her from the corner of its eye. She crosses to the window and looks out, anything to avoid looking at the baby, and that is when she sees the boy again, down on the shore. Again, she can't tell whether he is facing her or not. He is held in silhouette, unmoving but for the faintest shimmer of his shirt when the wind picks up. Then he raises his hand and he waves at her and instinctively she waves back. Tomorrow she will wonder how he has seen her in the gloom of the bedroom.

The baby is screaming now, and she wanders around in circles, trying to soothe it back to sleep. She walks into the long corridor at the back of the house and strides up and down, up and down, the flagstones hard under her slippered feet. She goes into the bathroom and sees that Eric has still not cleared the blockage in the bath, and that the water remains, stagnant and grey, even though she has already removed the plug. Cursing him, and holding the wailing infant tight against her chest, she leans down and pokes a finger in the grime, feeling for the plughole. She can feel nothing, other than the water, thick around her fingers, and she assumes that the blockage must be lower down. She wipes her hand on her jeans and readjusts the baby who is lying flat against her chest, quiet now, but with its breath coming in rapid shallow gasps.

Much later, Ana finds herself sitting at the kitchen table. Her laptop is open and her fingers are dancing over the keyboard, bouncing and caressing, and words are appearing on the screen that are not her words, yet somehow they are. She's reminded of those early mornings, lying in bed before reaching full consciousness, when the fully formed sentences would alight in her mind like butterflies, but would then flutter away before she could grab her notebook. Now, the words – hers or someone else's – are appearing on the screen, never to be lost. It is as though a tap has been turned on and the words are gushing out, her fingers flying to keep up with them. She has no sense of their totality, of what all the words will mean when they are collected into a sentence, of what all the sentences will mean when they form a paragraph, but she knows that it will be good. Not just good, but breathtaking and, for now, it is enough to know that she is writing again, and so it takes her a moment to realise that there is something else there, on the periphery of her attention. It's a voice, a small, high-pitched voice that swims in and out of her consciousness, and she struggles to block it out and carry on writing, anything not to stem the flow that she has missed so much in the last months.

But it's no good; she feels the torrent of words drying up as the voice invades her mind. She can feel a presence behind her, and without looking she knows it's Isaac. She won't turn around, she can't turn around, for to do so will break the spell, but she knows that it has already been broken as the first words her son has ever said to her finally attach themselves to her brain and she hears them properly.

'Who put the baby in the bath, Mummy? Who put the baby in the bath?'

The clatter of her chair hitting the flagstones is loud and her legs are heavy as she makes for the long, long corridor at the back of the house.

Badgerface

Dod's back and he's looking meaner than ever. He's come straight to the pub and even though I'm working he grabs me in a headlock and rubs his fist against my crew cut, and it hurts but I can't say anything so I just close my eyes really tight. When he's finished, he swings me round and puts his hands on my shoulders in a 'let me look at you' kind of way. His neck is short and wide and the tendons are sticking out, taut like ropes.

'Haven't got any less ugly, have you, Badge?' he says. When he's finished looking at me he lets me go and walks straight over to the bar and asks Sandra for a pint of Felinfoel. He drinks it down in one go and asks for another and I know it's going to be one of those nights.

In the six months that Dod's been gone, he's become enormous. His arms are huge, the muscles bulging from under the sleeves of his khaki t-shirt, swelling the tattoos and disfiguring them. The snake has become a python, not the elegant black mamba it was when he left, and the graceful bluebird has turned into a massive, irate eagle. There's an angel that sits on his shoulder, her arms stretching up into his sleeve, and even though I can't see it, I know that she's holding a harp above her head. She's swollen taut across his biceps, and looks more pregnant than devout. Even his thighs are straining against the material of his combat trousers. I wonder why he's come here in his work clothes, why he doesn't put on a track suit or jeans like all the other men in the village, but then I look over to where he's standing against the bar, halfway down his second pint, the flotsam and jetsam of the Ceffyl Du floating around him and I know why he's done this. The Hero's Return. He's getting pats on the back and shots of whisky bought for him, and Sandra's undone the top button of her blouse in celebration. I pick up the rest of the glasses and push my way through the throngs of well-wishers and put the pint pots down on the bar. There are still paper ghosts hanging up on the shelf behind, even though Halloween was yesterday.

'Bless him,' Sandra says in my direction, looking sad and disgusted at the same time. Dod catches my eye and winks and holds up his pint to me in a tiny salute.

When I get home, Darren's sitting on his own in the kitchen. He's chugging on a can of Stella and a Marlboro Light and I know Mam'll kill him if she finds out. I nod at him and fetch a can from the fridge. I sit down opposite and wait for him to speak. He doesn't, so I decide to get in first.

'Dod's back.'

Still he doesn't say anything. He stares at me for a while then he takes another swig of lager and pokes his fag end into the hole in the top. He crushes the can in his hand. He chucks it on the table.

'It's alright, Champ,' he says and he walks out. He's the only one who calls me Champ. Everyone else calls me Badgerface. Apart from Mam, who calls me by my proper name.

I open the top part of the window and flap my hand to clear the smoke and then I wrap his can up in a Spar bag and push it down the side of the kitchen bin. Then I sit there, drinking my beer and thinking about nothing.

I hear Dod get in sometime in the early hours. The pylons have been buzzing again, and I've been awake on and off even before the front door smashes open against the wall. Tonight the pylons are louder than usual, and I find myself wondering if this is because Dod's back. Then I tell myself that's stupid, and that's when I hear the door crash open.

There's the sound of a scuffle, and I think it's probably Dod falling over onto the pile of shoes and coats in the hall. The landing light goes on, and I know it'll be Mam. She's been fretting about today. Ever since he phoned to say he was coming back she's been jumpy, cleaning the house even more than usual, making sure there are fresh sheets on the bed and playing Shirley Bassey extra loud. She's had her roots done and her nails are all silvery-pink. Now I can hear them in the hall, and she's shushing him and he's coughing and then they're quiet for a moment. Kissing, I think.

'Baby Doll.' Dod thinks he's whispering but he's too drunk to talk quietly and Mam's shushing him again. Mam's got a frilly nightie, a baby doll nightie, and that's what Dod calls her in the first week when he gets home, after he's been away on ops. It's all 'Baby Doll' in the first week when they can't keep their hands off each other, and they lock themselves in their room for hours at a time, and Dod'll come out now and again to hand me a couple of twenties and an order for the Chinese and the offy. It's Baby Doll for the first week.

For the second week it's 'You Slag'. For that week they'll just fight and shout and Mam will start wearing more make-up under her eyes and sit at the kitchen table in her dressing gown, staring at her fingernails and picking away at the nail polish. She'll spend more time on the phone to Auntie Gaynor, and when she puts the phone down, she'll still be crying. That's the second phase, the You Slag phase.

Then it's just pure indifference, for both of them. It's as though they don't even know that the other one is there and they exist in two isolated versions of reality, getting their own food, making their own cups of tea. They'll go out separately, him to the Ceff, her with the girls, and they won't even tell the other one where they're going. Ships that pass in the night, Darren calls them.

Dod is crying now, loud sniffles that Mam is doing her best to soothe.

I wonder if Darren can hear them from his room, or if he's fast asleep.

In the morning, I push Darren's door open and go in without knocking, but he's already gone and his bed is made, the duvet cover flat and smooth. I think about lying on it, putting my head on his pillow and making an indentation there, leaving the shape of my head on the pristine surface. I can't do it though, and instead I pick up his aftershave from the chest of drawers and spray a bit on my neck. Davidoff Cool Water. Now I smell just like Darren.

When I get to the pub for the start of my shift, it's already kicking off. It's over soon enough, mind. Sandra doesn't take any shit and she'll chuck someone out on their ear soon as look at them, even if it's Jamie, who's Rabby's son and thinks he owns the place. Jamie's been going to the gym for the last few months, and I think he's been doing steroids, because he's massive and he's got this glassy look in his eyes that doesn't come from four pints of lager top.

When Jamie's left and it's all calmed down again, Sandra stands behind the bar, wiping glasses out with a cloth. She's hard as nails is Sandra. She has to be, really, to handle people like Jamie who'll smack anyone, doesn't matter if they're a man or a woman. Sandra's short and wiry, with dyed blonde hair in a tight ponytail on top of her head. Even though she's really old – late forties or even early fifties – she always wears a low-cut top, and you can see the tops of her tits hanging down inside, the skin brown and wrinkled, like potato peelings. Tommo said he got off with her once when he was off his face and she was closing up after a lock-in. He says he doesn't remember much about it but that she was really up for it and just the thought of it makes my stomach turn over.

Sandra's what you'd call a functioning alcoholic. She's not meant to drink on the job. It's illegal to be drunk and be in charge of a bar, but she's found a way round that. She'll get Alison to go to the optic right at the end and stick a couple of shots of Malibu into a glass of Coke. I don't know if Malibu has always been Sandra's drink of choice, or if she's chosen it because it's at the end of the optics, the one that's out of range of the CCTV camera, and so she can't be seen by Rabby who sits in the flat upstairs all night, just watching the footage of what's going on in his pub.

Dod comes in and goes to sit at the corner table. He catches Sandra's eye on the way through and she pours him a pint and brings it over and puts it on the table without saying a word. She gives him a half-smile, a sympathetic sort of smile. The celebrations are over. The hero has returned and now it's back to normal. I know that now he's back Dod will start to shrink. I know that the bulk he's built up while he's been in Afghanistan will start to shift; he can't keep it up when he's at home. Over the next six months he'll get smaller and smaller. He'll go back to wearing his jeans or his tracky bottoms. He'll cover up the tattoos, the snake and the bird and the angel, and he'll wander around, glass-eyed and morose, until Mam makes him phone up the PTSD counsellor and arrange some more sessions. That's how it always is.

Dod's finished his pint and he gets up and walks over to the bar. Instead of ordering another drink, though, he leans over and whispers something in Sandra's ear. She nods, biting her lip, and then she grabs a bottle of vodka from the store and lifts the flap at the end of the bar and walks through and Dod follows her over to the door in the corner. She keys in the code and Dod follows her through and the door shuts behind them.

When I turn back round to go and collect Dod's glass, I see Darren sitting in Dod's place. Darren never comes into the pub and I think that something's wrong, that something bad's happened, maybe to Mam, but Darren just smiles at me and gives me a thumbs up and his mouth makes the shape of 'Alright, Champ?'

Darren and Jamie were thick as thieves over the summer, virtually inseparable. Like Siamese twins, they were. For weeks, ever since they finished their GCSEs, they'd lock themselves away in Darren's room with the curtains shut, and it was only the sound of *Grand Theft Auto* crashing out from under the door that told anyone they were in there. Even Tommo and Justin Probert couldn't persuade them to go into town. Eventually Mam said that was enough, that they needed to get out and get some fresh air and she went in and opened the curtains and turned off the Xbox. 'And start looking for a bloody job, while you're at it,' she said as they sloped off down the path. And then she sat on the sofa and cried.

Dod had only been gone for a month by then, and wouldn't be back for another five at least. Mam always found it hardest at the beginning, when he first went off on ops, because she had to readjust to being on her own again. I told her that she wasn't on her own, that she had me and Darren, and she smiled at that, and gave me a cwtch, and then her eyes went all watery, and she reached out a shaky hand and traced it down the middle of my face, all the way down my birthmark, between my eyes and over my nose and my mouth and all the way down to my chin. I knew that after another couple of weeks she'd get herself together, get used to Dod being away, but I told her that, for now, Darren and I would look after her.

I caught up with Darren and Jamie about half an hour later, and in that time they'd managed to pick up Tommo and Justin Probert and a carrier bag full of cans from the offy.

The thing about Darren and the lads is that they had a pecking order, just like Mam's chickens. Darren was always at the top, just because he was the best of them all: the cleverest, the best looking, and the most successful with the few girls in the village that were worth getting off with. Jamie came next, but only cos his dad owned the pub and he could get them served. He looks like Wayne Rooney. Then it was a toss-up between Tommo and Justin Probert. Tommo's not bad to look at but he's thick as shit and his dad drives the lorry for the sewage works, so he and his sister always smell of shit as well. I don't mind him though; he's always good for a bit of banter and usually has a good story. Justin Probert is a chopsy little twat, and he's always picking away at his acne and hacking into a tissue. Still, he's the only one of them that has a job, or near enough to a job. He's got an apprenticeship at the butcher's on Swan Road, and he always seems to have a smell of offal about him. So it's shit or guts, if you're one of Darren's mates.

They were fifty metres or so ahead of me on the path when I spotted them, but I'd recognise Darren anywhere. He was the tallest of the lot, and he had a white t-shirt on, so bright and clean that it looked luminous in the sunlight. I knew they'd be heading for the pylons and I kept my distance so they couldn't see me, or they'd tell me to go back. I ducked in and out of the hedge, sometimes crawling on my stomach across the ground, commando-style, pretending I was Dod in the desert in Afghanistan. The grass under my belly was scratchy and crisp and dry.

Badgerface

The lads stopped when they got to the far pylon and I knew they'd chosen that one just in case Mam came to hang the washing out and saw them sitting on the grass with their cans and fags. The far pylon was the one Darren and I had always gone to when we were kids, and I knew that if I crouched down in the tiny copse of trees just next to it I'd be completely hidden.

Tommo and Justin Probert had cracked open a couple of cans, and were chasing each other like girls, giggling and splashing lager everywhere. Darren and Jamie sat side by side on the grass, leaning back on their hands, watching them. Not looking at each other.

I wasn't sure, I couldn't see properly through the leaves, but I thought that their fingers might have been touching in the grass. They carried on not looking at each other.

Tommo and Justin Probert started shrieking, their shirts stuck to their chests with Special Brew, completely oblivious to anyone else.

Then Jamie pulled his hand away and took out a packet of fags from the carrier bag and undid the cellophane. He pulled out the foil and tapped a cigarette out. Without asking, without offering, he turned to Darren and placed it in his mouth, and my brother's lips closed softly around it. Jamie pulled his lighter out from his back pocket. He cupped a hand round the flame and held it in front of the cigarette, waiting for Darren to take a drag. My brother put his hand over Jamie's, steadying it, and that's when I knew. I just knew.

I was out from behind the trees in a second.

'Fucking hell, Darren! Just wait till Dod finds out. He'll fucking skin you alive!' I don't know if I was angry or sad or just confused, but I ran at Darren and started hitting him, clobbering him over the face and head, throwing punches that were as weak as they were badly aimed. He pushed me away and jumped to his feet and grabbed my hands and held them down by my sides. Tommo and Justin Probert had stopped chasing each other and were watching us, frowning.

'Dod doesn't need to know, does he, Champ? Dod doesn't need to know anything.' Darren was whispering. Jamie wasn't even looking at us. He was looking away, lighting his own cigarette with shaking hands.

'Fuck, Darren, he'll find out.' I was whispering now, as well, aware of Tommo and Justin Probert heading back over to where we were standing, getting closer all the time. 'You know he'll find out. He finds out about everything in the village. Even when he's away.'

That's when Jamie jumped to his feet. He grabbed me by the collar and yanked me towards him. His teeth were mostly brown, the gums swollen and red around them, and his breath stank. I thought about him and Darren kissing and I felt sick. Jamie was filthy compared to Darren. He didn't deserve Darren. No-one did.

'He won't find out, will he, Badge? He won't find out because you're not going to tell anyone, are you?' He's quite big, is Jamie. Not really big like Dod, but short and stocky with broad shoulders and a chest like a tree trunk.

I don't remember how I got away from him, but the next thing I knew I was legging it over to the pylon. I'd climbed it before, loads of times, so I knew the exact combination of hand-over-hand movements I needed to pull myself up. I didn't look down until I was halfway up, a good twenty metres in the air, and then I saw that Jamie was still near the bottom, struggling to get a grip on the rails. Darren was standing below him, pleading with him to stop being such a dick.

Finally, Jamie seemed to relent, and slowly he climbed back down. Darren said something to him, something I couldn't hear, and then he was climbing up, one hand after the other, just like he'd shown me when we were kids.

When he got up next to me, he wiped the palm of his hand over his forehead. He wasn't as fit as he used to be. Fags and lager, I guessed, and his white t-shirt was grubby and sweat-stained. I wanted him to be the first to say something, so I waited and I leant back and looked over towards our house and there was Mam, standing on the back step, holding her dressing gown closed with one hand and clutching a cup of tea with the other, watching her chickens scratching in the dust. I wasn't sure if I could really see the dark shadows under her eyes and the wrinkles on her forehead, or if I could only see them because I knew they were there.

'Champ,' said Darren when he'd got his breath back, and he put a hand on my shoulder. We'd been up this pylon so many times that it felt natural to be there now. We belonged there, me and Darren, we were safe up there, away from everyone else. 'Champ, it's nothing. I promise. Nothing that Dod needs to know about, anyway.' I nodded, pleased that Darren wasn't cross with me.

'You won't tell Rabby, either?'

I shook my head. I didn't know much about Jamie's dad then. It was before I'd started working at the pub. I just knew that he had a reputation for being in with a bad crowd and he wasn't someone you'd mess with.

'Thanks, Champ.' We stood like that for a bit, our feet spread wide on the crossbar of the pylon, Darren with his hand on my shoulder, and I liked the feeling of it, heavy and warm and reassuring.

'Want to see something?' He was grinning now, and he took his hand off my shoulder and started rolling up the sleeve of his t-shirt. First feet, then legs and then a body and feathered wings appeared, and then a face with long hair and a halo, and above them, arms and hands holding a harp. It was the exact same design as Dod's tattoo. It was red around the edges, and looked sore and recent. He grinned at me. 'Tidy, eh? Just wait till Dod gets back. He'll love it.'

'Mam'll kill you,' I said, knowing I was stating the obvious.

'That's why I haven't told her.' Then he said, 'There she is,' and I looked down to where Mam was still standing on the back step. She'd put her mug down and was waving her arms at us in a gesture that said, 'Get down from there.'

'It's alright!' Darren shouted to her. He lifted his arm up, the one with the tattoo, to wave back, and that's when he fell.

Twenty metres doesn't seem so high when you're climbing. It's over in a flash, especially when you've got Jamie coming after you. But on the way down, it's a different story. Darren seemed to fall for minutes, his white t-shirt stark against the dirty yellow grass, and Jamie and Tommo and Justin Probert just watched him, their mouths open, their hands up, clutching at their hair.

*

When Dod and Sandra come back down from the flat, the pub's quiet. I've collected all the empty glasses and put them in the dishwasher and Alison's refilling the optics. I'm leaning on the bar, working my way through a packet of pork scratchings, but when I see Dod I scrunch up the packet and put it in my back pocket and pretend to be straightening the bar mats.

He's making for the door, and he doesn't even look at me, but I can see his eyes and they're red, like he's been crying. I look at Sandra, and she's bent over the dishwasher. I can't see her eyes, but there's something about the way she's holding herself, her shoulders slumped, her hair coming loose from her ponytail, that tells me she's been crying as well.

As Dod draws even with me, I can see the angel tattoo on his biceps. His sleeve's been rucked up, and I can see the top of his arm, the bulge of the muscle obscene. It's so much bigger than Darren's angel. Now I can see that Dod's tattoo has changed, that it's been altered while he's been away. It's not just bigger; now the harp has gone and the angel is holding a scroll above her head, a piece of paper that curls in her hands, the edges beautifully shaded to make them look 3D. On the scroll, in perfect, fluid script, are the words, 'Darren 1999–2017.'

I close my eyes and I put my hand up to my face and trace my fingers down, between my eyes and over my nose and my mouth, as far as my chin. When I open my eyes I can see Darren, sitting at the table in the corner, and his white t-shirt is luminous in the gloom of the pub. He gives me a big, double, thumbs up.

'It's alright, Champ. It's alright.'

The Pickling Jar

When the diagnosis came through, Gaynor was sad, of course. She and Dave had been married for twenty-odd years, and they'd been good years, despite him not being able to produce children. They'd sat in the doctor's waiting room, comfortable in their silence, both knowing what the test results would say. She'd picked up an old copy of *Good Housekeeping*, and the piccalilli recipe she chanced upon had seemed like a sign. She'd looked around, and then she'd taken her phone from her bag and photographed the page. The rules said that you weren't allowed to start the preparation straight away, just after a diagnosis, but they said nothing about research and she told herself that this wasn't preparation – especially if she didn't look at the photo just yet – but it might come in useful later.

When the doctor came to call them through, his face was already arranged into a mask of sympathy. They'd both cried a little when he told them it was only a matter of months, and on the way to the bus stop she'd wondered if it really was the right thing to do – to call in to the library and take out the recipe books. But Dave had told her to go ahead, to just go right in and get the books and he'd wait outside. He was always good like that.

They'd made all the phone calls that evening: family first, and then friends. No-one had been particularly surprised; Dave had been losing weight for months and his cough had become intolerable.

'You'll be wanting the pickling jar then, I suppose,' was Chloe Powell's response to being told the news. Gaynor had always suspected that Chloe was a bit of a bitch, but she'd tried to give her the benefit of the doubt after her husband passed away earlier in the year. That had come as a shock to everyone. Mark had been a personal trainer at the gym in town and was as buff as they come. He'd once made a pass at Gaynor at the community centre barbecue, leaning in over her, his lager slopping from the plastic glass as he whispered something rude in her left ear. She still wished she'd known what he'd said, wished that he'd been leaning into her right ear, her good ear, but it remained a mystery. The only way she'd known it was rude was the way he'd licked her earlobe with the tip of his tongue.

Three months later Mark was dead in a motorbike accident, and then it had been Chloe's turn to have the pickling jar. She'd had to collect it from Janet Evans, whose husband Ivor had fallen off a ladder the previous spring, while attempting to weed her hanging basket.

The pickling jar was a fairly straightforward thing. It held

The Pickling Jar

two litres and had a rubber ring around the lip, and a metal clasp that held the lid closed. Bryony Morris had bought it in TK Maxx after the last pickling jar had ended up on the white elephant table at the Christmas bring-and-buy. No-one was directly accused, but there were more than a couple of fingers pointed in Bryony's direction for allowing it to be on the table in the first place, and then for letting it be sold to the lady from the mobile hairdressers.

There had been a suggestion made at one of the WI meetings that they should update the rules, and be allowed to use the little jars, so that the pickle could be made in smaller batches and shared around the village, as a gesture of goodwill for those who were unable to attend the funeral party. This would also be more hygienic, Martha Davies had pointed out. But this had been voted down as too disrespectful, verging on the tasteless, and they had continued with the age-old tradition of preparing one big jar. As far as Gaynor knew, they only still pickled on this side of the valley; all the other villages had given up and now had other arrangements in place for their funeral parties. A shame to let go of traditions like that, said Mr Brewer from the funeral parlour when Gaynor had asked him about it. When they were gone, they were gone, he'd said, and you'd never get them back.

The months after Dave's diagnosis were a whirlwind of pickling research for Gaynor. She kept on renewing the library books, testing out different recipes and tweaking the ingredients each time. Of course, she had to make do with pork in place of the real thing, so none of her experiments were ever going to taste exactly like the finished article. She was a good and dutiful wife, though, so she still found time to take Dave his tea in the morning and to let in the Macmillan nurse. She even managed to go and visit him when he went to the hospice. Not every day, mind, as it was on the other side of town, but a couple of times a week. Towards the end, it didn't really matter anyway, as he wasn't himself by then.

Gaynor had made a point of not watching *Bake Off* after it moved to Channel Four, but she'd kept all the old episodes on the Sky Box, all the ones with Mary Berry and Mel and Sue. She liked Mary Berry; you knew where you were with Mary. She remembered one particular episode, where the showstopper was to be an enormous pork pie with raised sides, the pork filling topped with a meat jelly. One bloke had made a chutney to go with it that Mary had described as 'heart-stoppingly good'. Gaynor worked her way through each episode, fast-forwarding through the cakes and the biscuits, the meringues and the tarts. When she found the episode she was after, and had settled down with her laptop to take notes, she was disappointed to find that the man had actually made a ketchup, rather than a chutney.

The rules stated that pickles, chutneys and relishes were all allowed, but jams, ketchups and oil-based preserves were not. No-one really remembered who had come up with the rules; everybody just knew them. Not that long ago, Joyce Maynard had tried to inveigle a ketchup in under the guise of a chutney, but she'd been found out straight away when Mr Brewer, who was always the judge, had said that it had no discernible chunks in it. She'd blended it all smooth in the Magimix, the idiot, and had been disqualified.

Gaynor spent the weeks of Dave's rapid demise chopping and boiling, tasting and seasoning. She soaked apricots in brandy, and boiled up raisins in apple juice she'd pressed herself. She ground the spices with a pestle and mortar, and, eager to get the exact combination of sweet and sour, she'd even made the hour-long round trip to the deli in town to get their special Chardonnay vinegar.

One day, when Dave was still lucid, he'd picked up her hand and looked into her eyes. He seemed to be having trouble speaking, so she'd raised the glass of water to his lips and he'd drunk a little bit and then she could have sworn that he'd said, 'Coriander.' While Ivor Evans had actually had it written into his will that Joyce should include ginger in his pickle – written it into his will! – it was good enough for Gaynor that Dave had merely spoken his favourite ingredient to her. There would be coriander, and lots of it.

Gaynor spent a fortune on coriander, dried and fresh, and she even started growing a little pot on the windowsill. She bought heritage tomatoes and organic gooseberries. She went to the farmers' market for new season garlic and tiny, perfect chillies. She took great pleasure in drawing a spoon across the bottom of the saucepan, waiting for a clear line to emerge to indicate that she'd achieved the correct consistency. She made notes on each of her attempts, each time tweaking the recipe infinitesimally, and then disposing of the result after it had been tasted so she could start again. She spent long minutes scrubbing the pans clean, ready for the next batch. She grew weary and irritated at the constant vinegar vapours, the onion eyes and the chilli fingers, yet still she persisted. Each day she roasted and then patiently ground the coriander seeds that were to be the centrepiece of her chutney.

Once Dave had finally passed away, Gaynor went to see

Mr Brewer to make the funeral party arrangements. He was a large man, but his heft belied the gentle, almost tender way he had with his hands. It was always difficult knowing where to take the meat from, he said. Usually, he would slice it from the calves or the thighs, places that wouldn't show in an open coffin yet were still meaty enough to retain some bite. That hadn't been an option for Mark Powell on his motorbike, of course, who'd suffered such damage to his legs that what tissue could be salvaged was mangled and mushy and wouldn't have stood up to the pickling process. In the end, Chloe had asked Mr Brewer to extricate Mark's testes, and they'd sat, forlorn, at the bottom of the two-litre jar, looking for all the world like a nearly-finished pot of pickled eggs on the counter of the Red Lion. She'd served them as canapés, thinly sliced and arranged on blinis from Waitrose.

Gaynor knew that the timing was tricky, knowing exactly when to remove the flesh so that it could be added to the prepared recipe. Too early, and the chutney ran the risk of coagulating and turning rancid. Too late, and there wouldn't be enough time for the meat to tenderise and absorb all the flavours. On the whole, Mr Brewer tended to get it just right, and he showed up on Gaynor's doorstep three weeks before the funeral party with a sympathetic smile and a little foil-wrapped package.

On the morning of the funeral party, Gaynor oversaw the decoration of the community centre with the bunting and balloons left over from the royal wedding. The parties were always held at the community centre, just like the bingo and the whist drives, and the children's discos, and the Easter egg hunt. The trestle tables were assembled and covered with crêpe paper tablecloths, and paper plates and napkins were arranged along their edges. Paper cups were set out around jugs of squash and metal buckets held bottles of lager for the gents, and white wine for the ladies.

Gradually, the villagers arrived, and they went straight up to look at Dave in his coffin on the little stage at the far end of the hall and pay their respects. Then they'd wander off and stand in small groups, chatting and laughing. The children raced around, getting under people's feet and causing them to raise their eyebrows and tut, but generally they were tolerated. This was no time for getting upset.

As the clock raced on, Gaynor braced herself and started to bring the food out from the kitchen. There were baguettes, sliced into chunks and piled into baskets borrowed from the Red Lion. There was butter, cut into little cubes, and chunks of Cheddar and Wensleydale. There were a few carrot sticks and some cucumber batons. It was plain food, designed as accompaniments, rather than as a centrepiece.

The scoreboard had already been assembled at the far end of the hall. It dated back to the 1950s and by now listed almost a hundred names, painted freehand onto the blackboard surface. Of course, it wasn't the current Mr Brewer who had been the judge back when it had started, but his grandfather. The current Mr Brewer's father had been the judge for a brief period in the 1980s, until his tenure had ended abruptly with the unfortunate and accidental immersion of a hairdryer in the bath. (Mrs Brewer's chutney had been awarded an unprecedented nine-and-a-half points, which hadn't gone without comment.) Gaynor was sorely aware of the most recent entries, the ones written with the sort of pen that pubs use on the specials boards, pens that looked like chalk when they dried. She knew that Chloe Powell had got an eight, that Janet Evans had been given a seven-and-three-quarters, and that Joyce Maynard, with her wrinkly hands and lazy eye, had been awarded a big, fat zero.

At one o'clock exactly, Mr Brewer entered the hall and met Gaynor's gaze. She nodded at him.

'Ladies and gentlemen,' said Mr Brewer. 'Please take your seats.'

As the villagers found their places at the long table, Gaynor began to decant the chutney from the pickling jar onto saucers, which she then placed at intervals along the table. A couple of people leant forward and sniffed, and frowned, trying to guess the ingredients. A baby on its mother's knee slapped a hand into the plate on the table in front of it, causing a squelch and a ripple of laughter across the room.

Mr Brewer had adopted his customary position at the head of the table, and Gaynor placed a saucer in front of him.

'Thank you, Gaynor,' he said, and again she nodded. She stepped back and folded her hands in front of her and Mr Brewer picked up the little plastic teaspoon that sat next to the saucer.

Silence engulfed the community centre.

He scooped up a spoonful of the chutney. He raised it to his nose first, and closed his eyes and took in a deep breath through his nostrils, which he held for a couple of seconds before exhaling. Then, with his eyes still closed, he placed the spoon very deliberately into his mouth and closed his lips.

The Pickling Jar

Gaynor held her breath.

After a long moment Mr Brewer chewed and then he swallowed. He opened his eyes. He ran his tongue over his teeth. He put a finger to his mouth and slid it down between incisor and canine, dislodging a miniscule piece of something solid. Gaynor still didn't dare breathe, but made sure she was standing with her good ear turned towards him.

'It's good, Gaynor,' Mr Brewer said at last. 'It's very good.'

Gaynor let out her breath. Then Mr Brewer spoke again, and this time he wasn't able to meet her eye.

'It's good, but I think there's a touch too much coriander,' he told the tabletop. Gaynor heard a snort from Chloe Powell, and turned to see her smiling the smirk of the victor. With her good ear turned away from Mr Brewer, she didn't hear his final judgement, and the score she had been allocated, but she just knew.

All around her people were muttering and chattering.

Gaynor held back a sob and reached for a piece of baguette.

Cavities

By the time Olivia reaches the pedestrian crossing and prods at the button, the anaesthetic has taken effect. The hole in her jaw is gaping and consumes her tongue, and when she inserts the point of her little finger tentatively into the gap left by the molar, only her finger registers the space as wet and flaccid; her jaw remains numb. The hole feels bigger than it ought to, bigger than it should be possible for a tooth to fill.

'Ngggnggg.' That was all she'd been able to say, her mouth full of instruments and fingers, when the dentist asked if she was OK. 'Ngggnggg.' It didn't quite achieve the desired effect, and he'd just smiled and taken her nasal response as assent to carry on pulling. She'd been able to bear the pain – it had been more of a discomfort really – so she was glad she'd spared him embarrassment by saying that he hadn't waited long enough after the injection for it to really take effect. Besides, it was numb now, and that's what counted. She didn't like to make a fuss.

When she was little and her mother would take her to the dentist, she'd enjoy the sensation of chewing the inside of her mouth after they left, the sticker already curling on her jumper and the lolly sucked away and even the stick discarded. She'd chew and chew, relishing how the fleshy inside of her cheek would spring between her molars, numb. It would only be a couple of hours later, when the anaesthetic started to wear off, that she'd become aware of the damage she'd inflicted on herself. She's avoided the dentist for years, of course, putting up with the odd twinge and the accompanying bad breath for fear of fillings or extractions since she'd turned sixteen and was able to make up her own mind. But over the last few months, the pain in her jaw had become intolerable, and she'd had to grasp the nettle and register with a dentist.

When she arrives at the park, her usual bench by the pond has already been taken by a young woman. Early twenties probably, with her hair scraped into a tight ponytail at the top of her head. Denim jacket, jeggings, boots. She's looking at her phone, idly swiping with one finger while her toddler, androgynous in t-shirt and dungarees, runs in random arcs, chasing the ducks. There's a pram parked next to the woman, and the noise emitting from it is somewhere between a meow and a wail, and as Olivia sits on the opposite bench – the one that faces where she would normally sit – she is mildly surprised to see a tiny fist, fleshy and clenched, rather than a furry paw, lift from the pram and flail in the air before disappearing again. The woman does not look up from her phone, but she places a hand on the side of the pram and shoves it gently, causing it to rock. The intermittent squall from the baby diminishes.

Olivia places her handbag down next to her. She works her tongue around her ruined gum. She slides it into the hole where her tooth used to be. Her little finger touches the space and prods gently, then harder, daring the hole to open up and swallow it. It's a marvel how there's no sensation there at all, that the only feeling is in her fingertip, which tells her that the hole in her gum is doughy and wet.

She hasn't thought about Jason Edwards in twenty years. He had funny teeth, she remembers. There were too many of them, and the ones at the front all overlapped like dominoes that had fallen on top of each other, or the slats of a wooden fencing panel. They'd been brown like wood as well. She'd kissed him once. It was a dare, at someone's birthday party, and even though the thought had made her sick to her stomach, she hadn't wanted to hurt his feelings, so she'd puckered up and tried not to flinch as his tongue had worked its way around the inside of her mouth, lapping and probing.

She can't remember if it was at that party or another that she'd found the baby.

Of course, it wasn't a baby, as it turned out, but a doll that someone had floated face-down in the bath. She'd caught a glimpse of it as she entered the bathroom and she'd screamed and put her hand up to her chest. Two of the girls in the year above whose names she can't remember had laughed at her, and when they told everyone else at the party they'd all pointed at her and laughed at how gullible she'd been.

The toddler's crouched down at the side of the duck pond now, leaning forward and poking a stick into the water. The baby must have gone to sleep, as the mewling has ceased and the woman has stopped rocking the pram, and is gazing intently at her phone. Olivia can remember seeing on Facebook or Twitter an X-ray of a child's skull, the milk teeth still firmly in place, surrounded and boxed in by a swarm of adult-sized molars and canines, just waiting to crowd in and push the milk teeth out, desperate to take possession of that space. She imagines an X-ray of her own jaws, the hole where her tooth used to be just a great black void.

For weeks after the party, no-one at school had spoken to her. She'd been known as the girl who overreacted to everything, the drama queen who was easily upset. It was just before the summer holidays in the fourth form when things had got really out of hand, and the head had called in her parents.

She'd been sitting by herself at lunchtime, as usual, round the back of the Portakabins where she knew there would be no-one to torment her. She'd just finished her tuna sandwich and was balling up the cling film when she happened to glance up at the window of the domestic science block. The body was hanging at the window, the rope around its neck causing the head to fall forward obscenely onto its chest. The breath had left her lungs, and she'd tried to scream but had found herself silenced by her panic. She'd sprung to her feet, her hand up at her throat, and had started running in circles, not knowing what else to do. Her mind was blank, and she could barely breathe, and then she felt the warmth spilling down her thighs, and she saw the wet stain pooling on the tarmac, her knickers and her socks sodden and rancid.

That was when the fifth formers had sprung out from behind the Portakabin, laughing fit to burst, pointing fingers and a Polaroid camera at her. Jason Edwards had come running out of the domestic science block, loosening the fake noose from around his neck and grinning, his horrid brown teeth all jumbled together like shingle on a beach. Her panic had morphed into desperation then, and she'd fallen to the ground and curled into herself and cried.

The Polaroid had been photocopied and circulated around school for the rest of that week. Olivia hadn't returned. Over the summer holidays her parents decided to move to Cambridge where her father had been offered a promotion. She hadn't minded, really. In fact, she'd been glad to leave.

When Olivia wakes up, her shoulders jerk and she feels the faint dribble of saliva on her chin. Her first reaction is to look around to see if anyone has spotted her. She can see no-one at all; even the woman with the children has gone. She looks at her watch; she's missed her bus but there's another one in twenty minutes. She thinks she'll walk to the bus stop and wait there, rather than risk missing another one.

Her mouth is still numb, and her lips feel swollen and huge. When she touches them with a finger, though, they feel normal. She wonders about the dissonance between what she feels and reality. That's when she sees the leg sticking out of the shrubbery.

The leg is quite small, like that of a doll, and looks to be attached to a body, although she can't quite see, as it is obscured by leaves. She looks around, but no-one else is nearby. She is approaching the leg, already looking around for a stick with which to prod it, when a small smile lands on her lips. Of course. They are hiding, waiting for her to panic and shout for the police, for an ambulance. Then they'll take photos of her – or worse: these days, it'll be videos on their phones which will make their way onto the internet. Cautiously, not wanting them to know that she's cottoned on to them, she looks around her, surveying the bushes and the flower beds, and the little copse of trees that lies to her right. She knows that is where they'll be hiding, peering out from the darkness through the leaves, laughing at her. Well, she won't give them the satisfaction.

Without another look at the leg, she turns and makes her way across the path and through the gates and back onto the High Street. The woman from the park is running towards her, her ponytail bouncing, her eyes wide and wet. The pram bumps along jerkily in front of her.

'A little boy,' she says, breathless. 'A little boy. Have you seen a little boy? Two years old, this high.' She holds her hand down towards the ground, somewhere just above her knees. 'He's got dungarees on and a yellow t-shirt.'

Olivia thinks the woman is a good actress. She gives her a little tight-lipped smile.

'No. I haven't seen any children,' Olivia says, and feels a warm surge of pride at her own masterful handling of the situation. She recommences her walk to the bus stop, prodding the tip of her tongue into the hole in her jaw where her tooth used to be. She thinks the feeling is starting to come back.

Resting Bitch Face

The wife knows it's coming before it arrives. She can see it in his splayed-leg stance, the curl on his upper lip.

'Chewing wasps again, love?' The husband leans against the sink, a pear in his right hand.

'What?' But she knows what he's going to say.

'Resting bitch face. There was something about it on Facebook,' he says. 'Women get it all the time. It's when they don't think people are looking at them and they stop controlling their faces. They just let them hang and they look like they're having really evil thoughts, but that's just how their faces are.' He chuckles then takes a bite from the pear and the juice slides down his chin. 'Middle age, I suppose. Affects the muscles.' He wipes his chin with the back of his hand. For the first time she notices how fat his fingers have become.

'I'm forty-six,' she says. 'It's what my face does.'

He ignores her and picks up his phone, the pear dripping juice onto the lino.

The wife's early morning supermarket trips are essential for her sanity. She can browse the aisles in peace without the boy whining for sweets or the husband tutting at the price of things. When she's home and the car is put away in the garage and the shopping bags are dumped on the table, she starts to remove her coat. That's when she sees the thread trailing from the hem on the sleeve and she half-remembers feeling its tickle on the back of her hand when she was in the frozen food aisle, a strangely sensual pleasure she had enjoyed at the time, like the teasing flutter of a moth against her skin. Now the thread is coiled, serpentine and black, against the vulnerable white of her wrist. She wraps her index finger into it and coils it around, so the fleshy pad turns white and hardens. She yanks the thread and it snaps. She unwinds it and lets it fall to the floor. The blood seeps back to the end of her finger and turns it pink again. She can feel her coat sleeve dragging against the back of her hand, longer now, where the hem has come down. She should mend it, she thinks. She should go to the cupboard in the utility room and get the sewing kit and just do it straightaway. How long will it take? Five minutes? Ten? Instead she hangs the coat on the back of the door and puts the kettle on to boil.

She doesn't know how long she is sitting there before the boy bumbles in. He is crying and snivelling and rubbing his eyes, still sleepy. The husband follows him in and grunts in her direction before turning on the coffee machine. The boy stands, thumb jammed into mouth, and watches them silently. When he asks for eggs, one of the few words he knows, the husband obliges. The eggs slide, viscous, into the bowl. He retrieves the whisk from the drawer.

'What are you doing today?' he asks the wife, not looking up from the bowl.

The wife thinks she will say that today is the day that she must visit her father, but as she opens her mouth, the husband starts whisking. She closes her mouth. He stops and looks at her, expectant. She opens her mouth again and he resumes the whisking.

'Nothing,' she says, her voice consumed by the noise from the whisk.

The father's house is not the one she grew up in. It is a tired 1960s bungalow, vacant of sentiment. Its faded red bricks do little to brighten the neighbourhood and it is surrounded on all four sides by tarmac. Easy maintenance, he had said, in his usual desultory fashion.

Sometimes, when he's asleep, she thinks about killing him.

The care assistant's car is parked haphazardly in the driveway, and the wife (the daughter) reverse parks on the road. She is pleased with how she has manoeuvred her Corsa into a tiny space. When she first passed her driving test (at the fourth attempt, a handful of years ago), the father had laughed and told her that she shouldn't have bothered, that she'd never be able to drive properly, that she had no sense of space or direction. On one night out (their anniversary?) the husband had asked her, in his loud voice and in front of the in-laws, if she needed help getting into the parking space. The car park had been empty.

She lets herself in with her key. 'Hello,' she shouts down the hallway, then she readjusts her voice and phrases it as a question. 'Hello?'

There's no answer from the care assistant, so she wanders down the hall, looking in to the dining room on the left, the living room on the right. She's at the back of the house before she sees the father: slumped in his armchair in the conservatory, a white napkin tucked under his chin, and he's spooning day-glo orange soup into and around his mouth that she knows to be Campbell's Cream of Tomato – it's the only thing he'll eat. She can hear the care assistant now, rattling pans in the kitchen.

Later, she'll think that she might have found the nerve to send the care assistant back to whatever pitiful flat she could manage to rent on her zero-hours contract, and then she might have waited until the old bastard was asleep in his armchair. She might have fastidiously placed a cushion over his face and listened to his breathing becoming more laboured as he struggled to breathe. In-out, in-out. In. Out.

The house is quiet when she gets home, the husband at work, the boy at nursery. In the light from the bathroom cabinet the skin on her face settles into little folds here and there: under her eyes; the spaces on either side of her nose; the flap that hangs under her chin. She moves her head, adjusts her posture, and opens her eyes wide in an attempt to perk everything up, but that just has the effect of accentuating the wrinkles in her forehead, so she lets her face fall again. Resting bitch face it is, then.

She has considered plastic surgery, of course. The cutting, the stitching – did they still do that, or was it all injections now? – the swelling and bloating and the shiny, smooth-as-glass surface of the skin afterwards. The only time in her life that she has had stitches is after the C-section. She recalls the translucent thread they'd used to seal her body after removing the boy, the puckering of the skin around the wound, some plastic stuff the only thing that was holding together her womb, her muscles and her flesh. At the time, she would sit feeding the boy, his mouth clamped vice-like onto her nipple, and think about what would happen if the stitches burst. Would her insides just fall out, like some offal in an abattoir once a beast's underbelly is sliced through?

When the lesion across her abdomen became infected, she had thought of it as a sign of punishment – she was being called upon to pay penance for her dislike of the boy, and the pus that wept from the wound was there to remind her that she was a mother now, a putrid reminder of her new role. She thinks this is why the boy hates her.

She places her palms on her forehead and pulls upwards. She imagines a thread hooked into the skin on her cheekbones, and wonders how it would feel to pull it slowly, gently, so that the flesh on her face becomes taut again, regains its youthful suppleness. She can picture the needles – fish hooks they would need to be – that would allow this operation, to yank back her flesh and then to staple it – she can think of no better word – to her temples.

*

She fills the kettle and switches it on, then she takes off her coat. Without letting herself think about it, she goes to the cupboard and lifts down her sewing kit. The coat is black, so it is easy to find a thread that matches it and, squinting, she threads the needle.

She is an accomplished seamstress, having been made to take domestic science at school, rather than the woodwork and metalwork she wanted, and her stitches are small and neat and purposeful. When she has finished and the hem has been reattached, she ties a knot in the thread and lifts it to her mouth and severs it with her teeth.

The stab of the needle on the inside of her lip is merely pressure, not pain. She dabs with her finger at the puncture mark, but there is no blood. Tentatively, she prods the needle against the inside of her cheek. Again, she can feel the push of the needle against her flesh, but there is no discomfort or soreness. Bracing herself, she presses the needle into her cheek, and the slide of the metal through the skin is smooth and elegant: it glides. The needle is through to the other side, and she pulls it clear, all the way through. It draws the thread behind it, a dragging sensation through her flesh that both pleases and repulses her. The tail of the thread comes free from her cheek and she holds the needle between her finger and her thumb, the black thread glistening with saliva. She feels the same moth-wing tickle that she'd felt at the supermarket, but this time it covers her whole body.

She packs up the sewing kit and is replacing it in the cupboard when she remembers that it is time to pick the boy up from nursery.

*

Resting Bitch Face

The next day is a Saturday. The husband plays football on a Saturday.

'Fix this, would you,' he says, holding out his football jersey. He doesn't look at her; he's texting one of the lads.

She takes it from him, and sees that there is a small tear in one sleeve. Her tongue finds the place on her cheek where the needle went through. There is nothing there, no wound, no sore, but she has committed to memory the place where the tiny spike of metal entered and left her body.

'Wear the other one,' she tells him. 'I'll mend this while you're out.'

And that is how it begins. The sewing box is brought down, the needle is threaded and the puncturing begins. At first it is just one piercing at a time, the thrill of the metal sliding through flesh, the drag of the thread behind it, the marvel at the clear, unpuckered skin that's left behind. Soon, this is not enough and she turns the needle around and draws it back through her flesh again, creating a stitch through her cheek. She severs the thread and is satisfied by the feel of the rough cotton against her tongue. The stitch soon falls away, though, agitated by her probing tongue, so she reverses the stitch: the needle enters from the outside, is turned around and pushed back through. She ties the two loose ends in a knot on the outer side of her cheek and trims the ends fastidiously. Too obvious; it can be seen. She rethreads the needle with a pale pink thread that matches the colour of her skin. It is perfect. The resulting stitch is barely there, a small imperfection on her cheek, a tiny puckering. A dimple.

*

She visits her father the next day. The carer has called in sick, and there is no replacement available, so she heats the soup in the microwave and places it in front of him. His lips are white with flecks of god-knows-what, his bristled chin a receptacle for the orange drops. He utters no word of thanks and she imagines driving the needle through those sunken cheeks, puncturing the grey-whiskered lips, drawing the thread through, sealing them shut. In-out, in-out. In. Out.

The boy is in bed and the husband and wife are watching TV in the dark. When the adverts come on, the can of Stella he's resting on his belly is lit up by the bright colours, the highly coloured inducements to buy bouncing off the side of the can. It's the slight adjustment to his posture in her peripheral vision that tells her he's looking at her. He's going to say it, she thinks.

'Resting bitch face,' he says, and the accompanying chuckle makes the can bounce.

She considers telling him to fuck off, to take his fat belly and his can of Stella and just fuck off. But instead her tongue finds the stitches on the inside of her cheek – seven of them now – and cherishes each one in turn.

It is on the morning her father dies that she starts to feel the burning in her cheek. At first it is just a prickle, beads of heat that cause her skin to itch. By lunchtime, when she is sitting in the traffic jam that is mercifully slowing her progress to the hospital, the skin shows red and swollen in the rear-view mirror. The stitches have become subsumed by her flesh, pinprick dimples that pucker the skin; the effect is not unlike orange peel.

The care worker had phoned her just as she was feeding the boy. A massive heart attack in the night. She had found the father when she came to do breakfast in the morning. Face down, he was. Face down in a bowl of soup that he'd managed to warm up himself in the microwave and it was everywhere, all over his face and his PJs, like a bloody Jackson Pollock. The wife had smiled at that.

The funeral is quick and easy to organise, and it is a mere five days before the father is in the soil. By this time her cheek is distended, and the punctures are weeping a yellowish discharge. There is a waxiness to the skin, and it is slightly numb. When she wakes each morning, the pus has dried and formed amber crystals which lodge in the puckers made by the stitches. She has taken to lying on her back, the husband snoring next to her, and counting each stitch as she extracts the nugget of dried pus with her fingernail. It is crystalline on her tongue, and crunches between her teeth, before dissolving slowly into a fine silky liquid that slides down her throat.

The husband uses the wake as an excuse to get drunk – obscenely drunk – and an uncle has to help her get him out of the car and up the stairs to their bedroom where he is dropped onto the bed. He lies there, for all intents and purposes comatose. She treads quietly to the kitchen, where she takes down her sewing box and threads a needle. Good, strong, thick cotton, the one she bought especially to repair the tent last summer. The needle is long, with a wide eye, the hole large enough to accommodate the thread.

Back upstairs, she looks in on the boy. He is a lumpen mass under the duvet. As though he knows she is there, he wakes and starts to whimper, a sound which quickly turns into a whine, a noise which causes her to clench her jaw and brace herself. She tends to him.

The husband snores on their bed, starfished, his belly rising and falling along with his chest. There is a ragged gasping sound from his open mouth. She knows she must be very gentle when she purses his lips between her thumb and index finger to make the first piercing. In-out, in-out. He will wake gradually, the pain working its way through an alcoholic wall, and by the time he is conscious and aware of what she is doing to him, she will already have his lips stitched tightly together.

The Puckering

The creature's suckers are flat against the glass, circular, and slightly frilled towards the centre. The outer ring of each sucker is a paler shade of the grey-purple that clothes the octopus, almost lavender, and in the centre of each sucker is a hole, puckered, and gathered around the edge. The woman standing next to me sighs, a gossamer-light sound that is ruptured by the tapping of her finger on the glass, trying to get the animal's attention.

'They have three hearts, you know,' she says. She is still looking at the octopus as she speaks, her skin pink and luminous, like the inside of a shell, and her cheeks have a healthy bloom. The air around her is fresh with the gauzy tang of ozone. She turns to me, and the smile is slow, but when it comes, it fills her face. Tiny lines at the corners of her eyes appear, delicate creases in silk. My cheeks feel tight as I return her smile, too many years of exposure to the sea air etched into their contours.

'I'm sorry,' she says, and she gives a little shrug. 'I'm very fond of octopuses.' She flutters out a laugh, her teeth tiny and pearlescent. My teeth, when my tongue meets them, tell the story of years of neglect, their jagged edges meeting at peculiar angles. I turn back to the tank, soaking up the warmth of the woman's arm next to mine. Her familiarity is uplifting.

The octopus stares past us, the horizontal slits of its pupils like ancient buttonholes stitched into cloth. An appendage wafts in the water, sending particles skittering under the ultraviolet light, and another of its arms floats, equally graceful. The suckers that are attached to the glass in front of us shrink and detach themselves, one by one, in a slow act of seduction. The woman leans forward, both hands now flat against the surface of the tank. I long for the octopus to turn to her, to acknowledge her in some way, but it starts to drift away from us. In a sudden convulsion, it contracts its arms into its body, and then releases them, and the force causes it to shoot to the darker depths of the tank.

When I leave the aquarium the sky is the same hue as the concrete façade of the block of flats over the road: torpid, languishing, flat. Jammed onto the rocks of the west coast, assaulted by the Atlantic, once embraced by the Victorians as a summer refuge for the wan and the vain and those seeking succour from the smog of industrialisation, this town has long ceased to thrive. The last bastions of a seaside paragon have been allowed to crumble: first the funfair, and then the amusement arcade, followed swiftly by the ice-cream parlours. The hotels have succumbed to the same fate, the big houses along the esplanade reduced to cheap flats by anonymous property developers. Soon, the aquarium will close. This town has become a dour, ageing spinster, accepting of her inevitable demise.

The Puckering

I tell myself that I haven't been waiting for the woman, but when she appears I feel the skin of my arms puckering and my breath lightening. The air thrills with a current of change. She walks directly to me, as though we have arranged this meeting, and she stops two feet in front of me. She is slightly shorter than I am, and her hair is parted in the centre and falls to her shoulders, sleek and dark and gleaming. She glows.

'Three hearts,' she says. In that instant, I decide not to tell her I've worked at the aquarium for a dozen years, that I know more about the creatures of our oceans than most marine biologists. I decide not to tell her that I've lived in this town for all of my three decades, that I think I'll probably never leave now, how it's too late. I decide not to tell her about my husband, the fisherman, who is not cruel but is not kind either, or about our children, who have more in common with him than they do with me. I tell her none of this.

'Remarkable creatures,' I say, and she holds my gaze for a moment longer. She is a lightning strike of radiance in an overcast sky, and I am reminded that in beauty lies danger.

'Yes, we are, aren't we?' She hoists the strap of her bag over her shoulder, looks both ways, and crosses the road. I watch her until she turns the corner, her yellow blouse floating against the grey building a life buoy on a storm-livened sea. A man appears on a second-floor balcony and shakes out a rug, hazing the air with dust. He turns back to his door just as a toddler starts screaming.

That evening, my husband brings home a live lobster for tea. It is the length of his forearm, not including the pincers, which are held together at first with elastic bands, but then thrash wildly when he cuts them loose. Some people say that lobsters scream when they're boiled, but this one remains casually silent as the shiny carapace turns from sea-grey to pink to sunburn red.

My entire life has been spent in this cruelly indifferent coastal town. I had a father who worked the trawlers, like the other men: a brutal life on the sea, long days away punctuated by empty evenings, their vacuum filled with fists and ale. A mother who asserted herself against me and my brothers, but never against her husband, so that we bore the vicarious brunt of our father's temper. I was not a particularly bright child – and not attractive either, by all accounts – and my hostility made me a poor candidate for companionship. I was and still am a friend only to the rhythms of nature: the tides, the seasons, the allure that lies in their infallibility. The ocean.

As a child, I had an affinity with the sea and found solace in the shoreline. My early morning missions to comb the beach for things of beauty provided a sliver of nourishment in an otherwise starved adolescence. A perfectly intact oyster shell, its varnish holding all the colours of the sea; a nugget of coloured glass worn smooth by countless tides; a crab shell, the flesh picked clean by parasites, resting smooth in the curve of my palm. These objects I gathered into my pockets: trophies to bring colour to a lacklustre life.

My family make short work of the lobster, but I go to bed hungry that night. After my husband's breathing heavies, then settles into shallow grunts, I allow myself to fall asleep thinking of the woman from the aquarium, and I dream of feeding her oysters, her head thrown back, the juices spilling down her chin.

When I wake, it is dark, and I can still taste her salt.

My walk to work the next morning takes me along the esplanade, and for once I take time to examine my surroundings: the rusting filigree ironwork that encompasses the bandstand, home now only to broken glass and seagull shit; the skeletal ribs of the wooden benches, rotting into themselves. Even the scree path that leads down to the beach is weed-pocked and hostile. A life spent stagnant accelerates the process of decay.

The sun's touch on the back of my neck is soft and welcome, even though I know it is an unseasonal, transitory heat. The Ladder Rock, that ancient peril to the sea-bound, juts insistently into the horizon, beckoning in the same way that a train track draws one closer. As I approach the aquarium, I find my breath quickening, my steps becoming lighter. I tell myself that it is impatience I feel, not disappointment, when the woman is not there. I have waited long enough.

For the rest of the morning, a primary school group treks balefully around the tropical section, counting the minutes until they can assail the gift shop. *Octopus vulgaris* – the highlight of the establishment – remains sullenly in the depths of its tank, a flaccid mound of unmoving, speckled flesh the only clue that the inhabitant is the last common ancestor of humans and fish. The glass is sullied by myriad sticky fingerprints.

In trying to engage the children's imaginations, the teacher trots out the tales of our own coastline that have become limp with time: the smugglers who built a tunnel through the cliffs to sneak in the contraband brandy and who were buried alive when the roof fell in; pirates, convicted of treason and hanged by-the-grace-of-God from a gibbet in the town square. Each tale has been moulded by its retelling, like a sea-polished stone, and is intended to moralise; not open for interpretation, these stories are designed to instruct the children that dark acts are punishable. These tales are bereft of beauty, and the young faces remain impassive, bovine. They do not know the tale of the inhabitant of the Ladder Rock.

Lunchtime brings respite from the mundane; it is warm enough to eat outside, and I take my packed lunch to the bench on the esplanade. I take my time, positioning myself in the centre so as to deter any company, and take my sandwich from my bag. Mewling gulls circle.

The tiny islet sits a hundred feet from the shore, and when the tide is out, it is a soaring, barren place, the beach around it pocked with barnacle-clad humps of stone and rock pools. Now, however, the tide is in and the Ladder Rock towers implacably over water that is razored with waves, vicious white blades that stab at the heavens. The rock takes its name from the stepped surface that leads up diagonally to its pinnacle. Jagged and rough, it is only about twenty metres across, and no vegetation grows there, hampered in its germination by the chill north-westerly wind that howls in from the Atlantic. I have known since childhood that the only thing to inhabit the rock is the sea creature.

At first I had thought it was a seal, that sleek head emerging, gleaming, from the folds of water. Seals weren't uncommon back then, but it was rare to see one so close to shore. Shoulders emerged, and I'd thought it was a swimmer, an intrepid athlete who'd ignored the coastguard's warnings and chosen to take their chances in the water surrounding the rock. The currents there were notorious, an undertow that could pull a man below the surface and toy with him until the air abandoned his lungs and the water gained ingress. But then the woman pulled herself from the water, and I heard myself gasp as her hands gripped onto the sharp rock face, her arm-over-arm actions laboured and heavy. Hair, washed forward by the waves, lay in heavy strands and obscured her face, like sea wrack falling from the cliffs. I held my breath as the woman's torso emerged, pearl-pink and resplendent in its nakedness. With a hard-earned flex of her waist, she dragged her lower half from the water. The silver scales shone, tantalising against the dour grey of the rock.

I don't remember what happened after that. Did I move closer, clambering down the scree-lined path to the shore, or did I fumble for coins for the battered telescope to see her better? Did I stay to see how she moved, this creature from the sea? I have no recollection. Beyond the memory of that glistening tail and the long, dark hair that gleamed with the promise of the ocean, I have no other. Time has erased all trace.

I throw my lunch to the gulls, and return to the cosseting gloom of the aquarium.

Dawn paints the Ladder Rock with an agile brush, the contours of the cratered surface picked out in delicate coral-pink strokes.

Lucie McKnight Hardy

Last night we performed the charade of a family unit eating our tea. The herring he brought from the boat fell victim to my culinary skills, but nothing was said of it; the oily clag of fish hung over us as we ate in silence, my incompetence something to be anticipated. Their impassiveness was savage, and so – with an uncustomary impulsiveness – my decision was made.

This morning there is a glister in the air, and the bench I sit on still holds the lustre of frost. I wait for the first arc of the sun to peer above the horizon and then I stand and start to remove my shoes and my clothes, folding everything neatly into a pile. For once, I am not ashamed of my nudity and I take no pains to cover myself. The scree path is slippery underfoot, and the stones are cruel beneath my feet, but it doesn't take me long to reach the shore; the rocks become pebbles become sand.

The tide is encroaching; frivolous lacy edges suggest themselves to my toes as I place myself squarely on the sand. Its grit insinuates itself into my nakedness. My shins are smooth, the faint bruises telling tales of an erstwhile land-borne clumsiness. As the sun climbs, the sea comes to claim me; first my ankles and my calves, then my thighs and hips are caressed by the waves, the tidal pull lapping over and back, teasing: a suitor. I wait until I feel myself starting to lift, borne aloft by the ocean. My stomach clenches, the muscles tightening against the cold touch of the water, until I feel my breasts lift, buoyant, and the icy hand of the sea brushes over me, puckering my nipples.

I am suspended now, held entirely by the water's grasp. I might panic, think that it will not happen as I had hoped, that

The Puckering

I have been mistaken. But instead of turning and swimming for shore, I give my trust to the water and allow myself to float, and that is when I see her. At the pinnacle of the Ladder Rock, glowing in the dawn light. Skin as translucent and burnished, hair as sleek and gleaming, as when she appeared at the aquarium and came to claim me for herself and for the sea. Since my first sighting of her, all those years ago, I have known that I will join her. The expectation has been there all my life, a pocket of air in my soul that has kept me afloat.

I feel a new pliancy in my legs, as though the bones have become sinew. I flex them, testing their new musculature, and in doing so find that they have fused, become unified, and have gained a formidable strength. My fingers brush over the shiny surface of my tail, and I flick it, thrusting myself under the surface. The air in my lungs is quickly depleted, and then, miraculously, restored.

Parroting

The small boy enjoyed his visits to the old lady's flat. It was always warm and dark and smelt of violets. Just above the scent of violets, in that part of the spectrum where small boys' senses don't usually reach, there was a faint musky aroma, a smell that spoke of foreign countries, of warmer climates and rainforests. It was the smell that leached from the old lady's parrot.

The small boy had heard his neighbours speculating about how long the old lady had lived in the building. Some said that she had lived there forever, that she had been born there and that her parents had died young and suddenly. It was said that she'd fended for herself from an early age, and she had certainly lived without human company for as long as anyone could remember, keeping herself to herself and merely nodding sagely when greeted in the lift. She was ancient now, and frail, her white head sunk down between shoulders that were hunched and bony. Not one of the inhabitants of the apartment block could remember ever having exchanged a single word with the old lady.

The small boy had first become aware of the parrot one week day afternoon. He'd been off school with a fever that had burnt itself out by lunchtime, and as it had been a sunny day his mother had taken him to the park. Coming home, they had found themselves behind the old lady in the lift, her back stooped and her sharp, bony shoulders poking up through a bright blue silk shawl. They had shuffled around her to accommodate the many shopping bags that hung from her skinny arms. The bags bulged with strange and exotic fruits: some greenish yellow and large as footballs, some bright orange and small as fists, and others tiny and wrinkled and held in crinkled packages. There were bags of nuts and seeds too, but there were also biscuits and cakes, doughnuts and shortbread.

His mother – curiosity not being confined to small boys – had offered to carry the old lady's shopping from the mouth of the lift to the front door of her apartment, and the old lady had accepted with a gracious nod. As soon as her front door was opened the small boy had peered around the doorway while the old lady fumbled with her shopping.

And then he had seen the parrot.

It sat in a cage that was obviously too small for it. It was hunched over and had the tops of its wings drawn up around its head, as though it was trying to make itself smaller and escape the confines of its cage. Its feathers were glossy and starched, the blue and yellow vivid, even in the darkened room. As soon as the parrot saw the old lady it started squawking, a high-pitched screech that reached up to the apartment's high ceilings and echoed about the room.

The old lady seemed to forget about the small boy and his mother, and she hobbled towards the cage, surprisingly brisk for one so frail. She unlatched the door and pushed her bony arm towards the parrot. It looked at her for a moment, its head tilting left and right. Then, using its preposterous beak as a hook, it latched itself onto the old lady's yellow cardigan sleeve and hopped onto her arm. It shuffled sideways up onto her blue-silk shoulder and hunkered down, its beak jammed into the space behind her ear. Now it was cooing. The small boy thought it sounded a bit like a cat purring.

The old lady plucked a monkey nut from her cardigan pocket and offered it to the parrot. It gazed at her for a moment, its pupils dilating and contracting rapidly, like the beam from a lighthouse. The parrot reached forward and grasped the nut in its beak. The shiny, curved, top part of its beak closed over the nut, and the force of the hard cases coming together made the shell crack. Expertly, a hooked black tongue emerged, leathery but smooth, and spiked the kernel from the nut shell, which was discarded and fell to the floor. The small boy could not take his eyes from that tongue, its dry darkness suggesting a third, imposter, beak. He felt a new excitement, and wanted to stay longer, to see if the parrot would flash its lighthouse eyes again. He could feed it monkey nuts and stroke its feathers and maybe, just maybe, it would sit on his arm and coo for him too. And show its great black tongue.

He had felt a bit rude asking the old lady if he could stay and have tea with her, and had been surprised when she had nodded, her pleasure evident even though she did not speak.

His mother was reluctant at first, smiling and saying that they would come back another day to see the parrot. She even said that they had already made arrangements and promised to bring him back later in the week, but the small boy persisted, had even found himself able to shed a few tears, and the old lady smiled silently and beseechingly through blue-watered eyes.

Finally, his mother acquiesced, and the boy was allowed to stay for half an hour. His flat was only on the next floor up, and he was to climb the stairs and knock on the door as soon as he was finished having tea.

Now, several weeks and many visits later, a firm, if unusual, friendship had blossomed between him, the old lady and the parrot, and a comfortable routine was established. Each Saturday afternoon, once the small boy had done his geometry homework and his mother had gone for her lie down, he would take his place at the tea table once again. The bird, resplendent in its feathered suit of blue and yellow, would perch on the back of one of the elegant walnut chairs. It would regard him warily at first, as it always did, and then set about its business. First, it would select a fondant fancy and clutch it in its enormous claws while standing one-legged on the chair back. It would nibble delicately at the icing on top before devouring the sponge that lay beneath. Then it would attack a Jaffa cake, the orange jam smearing rudely across its beak. It would go for a flapjack, and the black horned tongue would curl out and hook the cake greedily, like a small finger, making sure it got all traces of the food in one go.

The small boy would smile at that. He enjoyed watching this exotic creature eating such everyday items. The old lady, cocooned in her warm, dark flat that smelt of violets and decay, enjoyed watching the small boy.

Parroting

And, even though the small boy never noticed, sometimes the old lady's tongue would pop out, leathery and black, and hook the crumbs from the corners of her mouth.

Cortona

The previous guests had evidently forgotten to put up the pigeon nets before they left. There is bird shit everywhere. Guano, she remembers from O-Level English, when her teacher had lost her temper half way through the lesson on *Lord of the Flies*.

'Does anyone know what guano is?' she had asked, and was met with a sea of slack-jawed fifteen-year-olds. Even now, thirty-odd years later, standing on a balcony in Tuscany, Rebecca can remember her teacher's sharp intake of breath, and the way the vein throbbed in her neck. She can't remember the teacher's name, but she can remember how she looked around the classroom and met the eye of every pupil in turn.

'Shit!' she'd shouted. 'It's shit. Guano means shit. Specifically, the shit of seabirds, birds that eat seaweed, but essentially it's just shit. Remember that for the exam.' Her outburst had been met by nervous giggles from the fifth form, and whispers behind hands. Three weeks later she went off on sick leave, and during the Easter holidays they heard that she'd been found by her husband, hanging from the light fitting in the spare bedroom. There never had been a question about bird shit in the exam paper.

Rebecca retrieves the broom from the cupboard under the stairs. Luckily, the warm temperatures have caused the guano – she'll think of it as guano, even though pigeons are not seabirds – to dry out and harden, and it comes away from the terracotta tiles in small, brittle chunks, like the forgotten pieces of Play-Doh she would sometimes find laid out on the shelves of the toy cupboard in Katie's bedroom.

She stands for a moment on the threshold of the balcony, the kitchen gloomy behind her. In the distance she can see Cortona, high up on the hill, and she knows that soon it will be lit up, the lights blinking in the evening haze in exactly the same way they have done on the eight previous occasions she's stayed here.

Up close she can smell the guano, and she wrinkles her nose as she sweeps it into neat piles. She notices that it has accumulated in one corner, under the shower-room windowsill that is set high up, at her shoulder level, and upon which sits a flowerpot. Even though she is tired after her journey – two hours with EasyJet from Bristol, and then another two hours in a rental car from Pisa airport – she feels that she can't settle into the apartment until she has made it clean and neat. She fetches the dustpan from under the sink and sweeps up all the little piles and places them into a carrier bag she finds in a drawer, the previous guests having emptied the place of bin bags.

She's pleased with her progress, and thinks she'll unfold one of the metal chairs and open the bottle of gin that she picked up in duty free. When she catches sight of the windowsill, where the guano has cascaded down the side of the flowerpot, she knows she won't rest until it has been cleaned. There is a small metal trowel on the floor of the balcony, one that is used to turn over the soil in the window boxes at the other end, and she picks it up and starts to scrape at the mess. She works methodically, and little nuggets of black and white fill the dustpan which she empties into the bag. When she is convinced that she can't scrape up any more, she thinks about the chair and the gin again, but it occurs to her that if she can just lift down the flowerpot, she will be able to clean away the few remaining smears and everything will be perfect.

The flowerpot isn't that big, really – about six inches in diameter – but it's quite tall and it's made out of chunky terracotta, with a floral pattern embellished on its side. She hooks her thumbs over the lip of the pot and starts to lift and feels the strain in her shoulders; she thinks it must be filled with soil to weigh this much. That's when she feels the warmth. She feels something warm and soft on her thumbs and she draws in her breath and says, 'Oh my God,' but she doesn't drop the pot. She can barely breathe but something tells her she mustn't drop the flowerpot and so she lowers it onto the little marble-topped table.

Two heads appear: dark, with large, bulbous eyes. Yellow fluff still clings to the beginnings of greasy grey feathers. The beaks are too large and heavy for the heads, which sway slightly on narrow necks. The chicks gaze at her, glass-eyed and indifferent. She takes a breath and reaches out a hand to touch their ugly heads, but something tells her not to. Surely they have a mother here somewhere, a source of food and warmth? She looks around but there are just too many of the creatures, hopping over the rooftops, perching on the TV aerials, the males courting the females with their woeful coos and splayed wings. She looks for a single bird, a pigeon watching her with an anxious expression, and she smiles at her own foolishness.

She replaces the flowerpot, careful to put it back in exactly the same position, and she washes her hands at the kitchen sink. She retrieves the gin from the see-through duty-free bag and unscrews the cap. She goes to the freezer for ice but sees that the previous tenants have left the ice-cube tray, empty, on the draining board. She pours two inches of tepid Bombay Sapphire into a tumbler and leans against the doorframe between the balcony and the kitchen.

The night is slowly coming in and the lights on the other side of the Val di Chiana are winking at her. Cortona is why she is here and tomorrow she will visit. In the meantime, she will drink her gin and read a bit of her book and turn in for the night. She raises her glass to her lips and that is when she smells it, ripe and warm and fruity. Fishy, too, like salmon a day past its best-before date. She takes a large swig of her drink and goes to wash her hands again.

It is mid afternoon before she heads down the hill to where she has left the rental car. She woke in the early hours, parched, and that is when she realised that she had forgotten to buy bottled water. The water from the tap is safe to drink, if unpleasant to taste, and she stuck her mouth under the tap in the shower room and slurped greedily. She went back to sleep, a dream-filled, fitful sleep, until midday, when she rose and showered, her head thumping.

Cortona

Before she leaves for Cortona she checks on the pigeon chicks. Still they eye her blankly and still there is no sign of the mother. She knows she will be out for a long time, and this will give the mother space and an opportunity to feed her offspring. Before she closes the balcony door behind her, she notices that the smell is different. The smell of shit is barely discernible now and has been replaced with the sweet, treacly scent of decay she smelt on her fingers last night.

The drive to Cortona takes her forty minutes. Even though the hilltop town is easily visible across the valley from the apartment's balcony, the route there is arduous, a meandering road that takes in several inconsequential villages along the way. It is only when the car starts the climb up the hillside, and the floor of the valley is laid out beneath her, that she allows herself to acknowledge the significance of her journey.

She parks in the municipal car park and heads straight for the Piazza della Repubblica. As she approaches Riccardo's café, she stops for a moment and watches him leaning against the counter. He is older, fatter and balder than he was last year. Eventually he turns, and although he knows the date and has been waiting for her, he stares at her for a long moment before recognition kicks in.

'Rebecca! Ciao, bellissima!' he exclaims, and holds his arms out to her. There are two crescents of sweat under his armpits, and she smells body odour and tobacco and coffee as he engulfs her. She is repulsed and comforted at the same time.

*

The church is at the very top of the hill, and is one of the oldest buildings in the town. An essential part of her journey is to walk there through the little square, from where Riccardo had called the ambulance, and had later retrieved the pushchair. At some point during the days that followed the accident, she had gone to the café for no reason and collected the mangled pushchair. By then she had no use for it anymore.

She pauses for a moment to catch her breath in the shade of a restaurant's canopy. That night had been the first time they'd slept together.

She recommences the climb.

The air in the church is mercifully cool and the pungent scent of incense is reassuring. Nothing here has changed. She stands in front of the life-sized sculpture of Santa Caterina. She fishes a one-euro coin from her purse and feeds it into the slot in the metal box. She selects a tea light, taking care to find one without a dented base or a scorched wick. She lights it from one of the other tea lights and places it on the stand. Even though it makes her self-conscious, she refuses to make the sign of the cross and sinks straight to her knees on the hard-stuffed stool.

She is not praying. It is the opposite. She is allowing her mind to empty of all thoughts and emotions. Here, in the shadow of Santa Caterina, she can truly empty her mind. For a few minutes, once a year, she is allowed to be numb. For a few minutes she is allowed to stop the recriminations and anger, without the need to manufacture petty distractions.

Riccardo is waiting for her at the café after she has made her way back down the steep cobbles to the piazza. She knows that later she will sleep with him, and it will be a perfunctory and unsatisfactory experience, and she will be at once removed from it and saddened by it, but it is a vital part of the pilgrimage. He was there.

Early the next morning, she leaves Riccardo sleeping, wheezing and muttering, and she gathers her clothes. She dresses in the bathroom and lets herself out into the cobbled street. The colours in the streets around her – terracotta tiles and garishly painted bowls on display in the tourist shops – are brighter than they should be and there's a wobble to the air, even though it's not yet hot. She half-heartedly wonders if she should be driving; her head is swimming and she feels nauseous. She lost count of the number of bottles of wine they'd worked their way through last night, first at the café and then at his grotty little flat upstairs. She barely remembers the sex, and is grateful.

She pulls out from the car park and steers carefully, aware of the alcohol still in her system, but accepting of it, as though fate will make its own choices. She is driving slowly, slower than she would normally, when the lorry pulls out in front of her.

Instantly, her foot is on the brake and the car stops abruptly. The lorry driver holds up an apologetic hand and she returns the wave, feeling pleased with herself at her swift reaction. By the time she gets to the car park in her village, half an hour later, her jubilance has worn off and she is aching, her hands cramped from gripping the steering wheel.

She is thankful when she can eventually abandon the car, and also when she sees that the small supermarket is already open. She buys a bottle of water and some chewing gum and gulps and chews her way up the steps to the alley, and then up more steps until she reaches the front door of the house. She lets herself in and stands for a moment in the welcome darkness of the hallway. Once she has regained her breath, she hauls herself up the steep stone staircase to the second floor, where she lets herself into the apartment, spits out the chewing gum and gets into bed.

The sunlight is very bright when she wakes, and she calculates that she must have been asleep for seven, maybe eight hours. It is mid afternoon, the hottest part of the day, and she can feel the sweat collecting on her forehead and bristling in the roots of her hair. She goes to the shower room, undresses, and climbs into the cramped cubicle. She lets the cold water run over her, through her hair and down her back, and imagines the accumulated dirt and grime being washed away.

From the corner of her eye she sees movement, and turns to the little high-set window. Outside, she can see the flowerpot, and the heads of the two chicks protruding, watching her. Even though the window is open a crack there is no smell of guano. She smiles at the chicks and feels fresher and cleaner than she has in years.

Later, as the sun is setting and the lights of Cortona start to twinkle across the valley, she will sit on the balcony drinking the last of the gin, still with no ice. She will stumble slightly as she stands and when she leans against the metal railing it will squeak in protest. She will talk softly to the chicks, pretending that she is their mother and has come to care for them, to help them grow and to show them how to fly. The drink makes her drowsy, and she'll sway softly to the words in her head of a song from eight years ago that they used to sing together. The balcony will squeak again. She'll think that the smell from the pigeon chicks, which was once putrid and cloying and rank, is actually pleasantly sweet and powdery, like the top of a baby's head.

Chooks Don't Have Teeth

The hen was making gentle plinking sounds as Marianne lifted it from the chicken house. She tucked it under her arm in a practised way and closed the hatch.

'Got to get her out every day. The bugger's gone broody and wants to sit in the coop all day, hatching out her eggs. Want to stroke her?'

Deborah reached out a cautious hand. She'd never touched a live chicken before. Its feathers were smooth and glossy, even though they were ruffled, and they were orange and black, just like its eye.

'She's all puffed up like that cos she's trying to protect her nest,' said Marianne. 'Look, she's plucked out all the feathers on her belly so she can get closer to the eggs. Keeps them warmer.' She tilted the bird, and Deborah could see a bald patch of white, puckered skin, just like on the chickens her mother would prepare for the Sunday roast.

149

Marianne strode across the yard and deposited the hen by the galvanised water drinker. It didn't drink straight away. It sank onto its belly in the dust, its wings slumped onto the ground, and regarded Deborah with its orange eye. The line that cut across its beak and into the flesh of its face – its mouth, Deborah supposed – was downturned.

'You feeling a bit better now?' Marianne asked.

Deborah nodded, and when she tried a smile she felt the dried tears tighten the skin around her eyes. She wrapped her fingers around her wrist, circling the red bracelet Callum had made there when he gave her the Chinese burn. Even though he was Marianne's son, Callum didn't speak like Marianne, with that lazy drawl, because he'd been born here, not in Australia. Deborah liked how Marianne was big and brash and tanned, with a wide face and short, straw-like hair. She was wide-waisted yet strong, and seemed to fill the yard, planted there solidly in a vest and shorts and filthy wellies.

Deborah – sweating in her too-tight party dress, her hair in a rigid plait – decided then that she liked Marianne very much.

'Your mum'll be here to pick you up in a little while. Why don't you go and carry on the party games with the other kids?'

Again, Deborah nodded, but when Marianne had turned away from her to fetch the chicken food, she found her voice and asked the question. 'Why don't you just let her sit there, if that's what she wants to do?'

Marianne turned back again, the metal scoop held club-like in one hand. ''Cos the bloody bird's a liability to herself. When they get like that, all they can do is sit and wait. They forget to eat and drink water. And they don't move around, so after a while they can't remember how their legs work.' Marianne smiled, displaying teeth that were strong and white. 'Sometimes, they just shrivel up and die.'

Deborah nodded to confirm she understood. She went to stand on the periphery of the game of hide-and-seek that was taking place in the orchard, so that when her mother arrived to collect her it would look like she was taking part.

Before Deborah went to bed that night, after she had brushed her teeth and given her hair one hundred strokes of the hairbrush, she knelt at the bottom of her bed and put her hands together. She said the Lord's Prayer, like she always did, but tonight she added on a little bit. She asked God to make her mother more like Marianne. Then she felt bolder and asked God if he could arrange for her to go and live with Marianne, instead of with her own mother, but then she felt disloyal so she asked God to cancel that request and go back to the original one.

When Deborah opened her eyes the next morning, she expected to see the yard at Marianne's house, with the chickens scratching in the dust, and the water butt, and the dirty tools lined up against the shed, just like in her dream. It was disappointing to wake to the mundane reality of her own bedroom. She lay in bed for a long while, revelling in the memory of Marianne's strong hands and her gentle way with the chickens.

Her mother was already in the kitchen when Deborah went down. The table was laid for breakfast for two, as it always was on a Sunday. Her mother was delicately built, with a tiny waist and a brittle collarbone. She would dart about in dark, neatly fitted garments designed to conceal what was underneath, and Deborah thought that she tried to inhabit as little of the space around her as she could. Deborah knew that her mother owned a pair of wellies – they were placed neatly side by side in the boot room – but they were always spotless.

The chicken had already been prepared, and it lay under a tea towel in its roasting tin, a lemon just visible, sticking out from its bottom. Deborah knew it would have had butter smeared onto its skin and salt and pepper and dried herbs – oregano and rosemary, probably – rubbed on top. Deborah also knew that after breakfast she and her mother would walk to the church in the village, where they would sit quietly through the service and then return home. By midday, when they sat down to eat their lunch, the chicken would be juicy and tender, the skin crispy and brown. They would eat it in silence.

Deborah touched her wrist and felt the dull ache where the raw skin had settled into a bruise.

For the next few weeks, Deborah watched *Neighbours* and *Home and Away* religiously. She practised her accent every night before she went to bed. (Was it wrong to recite the Lord's Prayer in an Australian accent, she wondered? She concluded that it must be OK, as that was how Australians did it.) She took a book out of the library and learnt about convicts and Sydney

Opera House and kangaroos, about how their babies were born and climbed up, through their mother's fur, and into the pouch on her tummy where they stayed for ten months, until they were big enough to leave. She wondered what it would be like to have a pouch on your tummy, with a baby in it.

It was almost the end of term before Deborah was able to see Marianne again. Every day since Callum's party she had thought of her, with her sturdy shoulders and kind eyes, and wished she could spend more time with her. She didn't wish ill on her mother, but she did wonder if there was some way she could engineer a situation where she would be taken into care, and Marianne would foster her. She didn't like the idea of living with Callum, so when she entertained these fantasies she made sure that he was in a borstal, or whatever those places were called now.

She'd calculated that the eggs would have hatched by the time they visited the farm, and she was right. When they got there, Marianne was standing in the middle of the yard, her shoulders broad and brown, a little lifebelt of fat filling the part of her vest that sat on the waistband of her cut-off jeans. She was surrounded by a hen and her brood of a dozen or so round and downy chicks. When she saw Deborah, she beckoned her over and showed her the chick crumbs she held in her hand. She poured some of them into Deborah's cupped palm and told her to hold it out to the chicks.

'Won't they bite me?' Deborah asked.

Marianne laughed. 'Don't be silly, darling! Chooks don't have teeth!'

Deborah had never been called darling before. It was as though a warm hand had settled on the back of her neck and she felt a glow spreading through her chest. Still, she looked at the sharp little beaks with suspicion and would not let them eat from her hand.

'A couple of weeks and we'll be able to sex them,' Marianne said.

'Sex?' Deborah blushed.

'That's right. Work out what sex they are. Tell the girls from the boys.'

Marianne stooped and grabbed one of the chicks. It let out a plaintive cheep, and its mother started strutting up and down next to Marianne's feet. Very gently, Marianne took Deborah's index finger and rubbed it across the top of the chick's head. Deborah felt a tiny, puckered ridge.

'That's its comb,' Marianne said. 'When they start to grow up, the cocks' combs get bigger and redder.'

'What happens to them? When they've grown up, I mean.'

'Well, the hens stay here and have chicks of their own. The cocks get dealt with. We can only have one cock at a time, you see, or they'd fight.'

'Dealt with?' asked Deborah.

'Yeah. Cruel to be kind, you know?'

Deborah nodded to confirm that she understood, even though she didn't.

The Easter holidays dragged their feet, and Deborah found even the twice-a-day Australian soap operas to be tedious. One day, when her mother was at work, Deborah turned off the television and made sure the front door was locked behind her. It was unseasonably hot, and she took off her cardigan and tied it around her waist, like the boys did at school with their jumpers. It was no distance at all to the café in the village, and she half hoped to see some of her classmates who hung out there, even though no-one had spoken to her since Callum's party. She was so bored by now that she would put up with any of their name-calling and petty violence, just to have some company. The café was empty, apart from an old lady with a shopping trolley, so Deborah bought herself a milkshake and sat down at the window.

She had finished her drink and was visiting the toilets at the back of the café before leaving when she noticed the rusty-red spotting in her pants. She didn't panic – they'd learnt about this at school – but she was curious and elated and excited, all at once, and she thought she should tell someone. She couldn't go to her mother's office; she knew that was only to be done in the case of emergencies, and this didn't count as an emergency. This was a momentous day, but not an emergency.

It was as she was wadding up some toilet paper to place in her pants that she thought of Marianne. Marianne with her kind face and firm but gentle hands. She would share her news of womanhood with Marianne.

The farm wasn't far; a couple of miles across the fields would take her to the top of the lane and from there it was a short walk to the farmhouse. By then, the sun was really very hot, and Deborah wondered if she should cover up her shoulders, or at least put on some sun cream. She could feel the skin prickling, and she pictured her shoulders, reddening and burning and turning crisp.

When she got to the farm she stood for a moment at the edge of the orchard. She could see Marianne sitting on a deck chair in the yard. Next to her was a trestle table, and on it a big pile of black and orange feathers. She had a chicken on her lap. Deborah squinted against the sun and held up a hand to shield her eyes. Marianne looked up at the movement.

'Hey, Deb. I'm just seeing to the chooks and then I'll get you a drink. You look parched.'

Deborah nodded, to show that she agreed, and stepped closer.

There were feet with claws hanging out from the pile of feathers on the table. At the other end of the pile, she could make out a few livid-red combs.

Marianne turned her attention back to the chicken on her lap and took its neck in her hands. The movement of Marianne's wrists was firm and graceful, and as she watched, Deborah's fingers found the place on her arm where even now the skin felt delicate and raw.

The Devil of Timanfaya

The villa is not nearly as big as it had looked on the website. The walls are still a blinding white, though, and the pool looks clean enough. It is in a nice area: mostly other villas, and a few restaurants and shops.

'Mummy, come and see this.' Henry is crouching down on the black gravel path that leads from the parking area. He has a stick in one hand and is pointing it at a cat. The cat is not like any other cat Tessa has seen before; it is white and very leggy with a wide face.

'Don't touch it, darling,' Tessa says to her son. 'It'll have fleas.' He ignores her and pokes the cat in the stomach with the end of the stick. She can't bring herself to admonish him.

The paved patio area is surrounded by black gravel, the volcanic rock that covers the island. She'd been surprised when Alistair had suggested Lanzarote: 'If it's good enough for the Camerons,' he'd said, 'it's good enough for us.' She'd winced at that. Alistair had been asleep when the plane started its descent, a thin trail of saliva leaking from the corner of his mouth, but she had seen the island from above: the inhospitable terrain, barren, and clinging to the coast, the relentless black sand.

They collected the hire car without incident, and drove for half an hour along the coast. All the way Amelia was on her phone, swiping and jabbing, typing rapidly with both thumbs and then a final triumphant tap before smiling to herself. Alistair thought that, at eleven, Amelia was too young for an iPhone, but Tessa had insisted. She enjoys indulging her children.

Later, they eat dinner at a restaurant in the village. It is adequate, but no more than that. Henry hadn't been able to eat his pork, it was too spicy, and they didn't have gluten-free pasta for Amelia, so she'd had to make do with a salad, which she'd hated.

As they return to the villa, and the car headlights swing around the corner, they light up the house on the opposite side of the road to theirs. She hadn't noticed when they'd arrived, but she sees now that the paintwork around the windows is scorched and blackened, and the windows themselves are boarded up. Even the door looks as though it has been burnt. She turns as they pull into their drive, taking one last look at it.

Alistair takes one hand off the steering wheel and places it on her knee. 'OK?' He shoots her a glance as he slides the car into the parking space.

'Fine,' she says. 'I was just looking at that house over there. Looks like there's been a fire.'

His hand is rubbing away at the flesh on the lower part of her thigh. She tries not to flinch.

'I'm sure it's nothing, love. Nothing to worry about.'

She knows he's protecting her. If she were to look at him, she'd see the concern in his frown; she'd see the bags under his eyes that have been there since she started being ill. Such a euphemism: 'being ill'. It's the term they've coined so that they don't have to mention anxiety, or panic attacks, or the deep, crushing terror that can engulf her at any moment, the dark tunnel down which she'll travel with no knowledge of when or if it will end. Nobody knows why the panic attacks started, or how to stop them. The doctor has taught her some coping techniques – deep breathing, focussing on the present moment, counting – all of which have had limited success. She still gets to the end of an attack not knowing how she has survived. The terror she feels is absolute and all-consuming.

'I'm fine,' she says, and removes his hand from her leg.

The night is coming in surprisingly quickly, and from where she is sitting on the patio, she can only just make out the shape of the burnt-out house on the other side of the road. Amelia has spent the last hour glued to her phone, texting and jabbing and swiping. Tessa has her arm around Henry, his head on her shoulder. She strokes his hair as he dozes. She pictures him as a baby, cocooned in her arms. He has always been so perfect, so small, so vulnerable. His pale eyelashes flutter as he sucks on his thumb. Alistair has tried to get him to stop by telling him that only babies suck their thumbs, but each time Henry cries and comes to her and she shushes him and tells him Daddy's being silly.

She watches Alistair as he flicks through the tourist leaflets that have been left for them on the coffee table, and is gratified to see that there is, actually, something of David Cameron about him: flaccid pink flesh, like bacon, and a chin that is sinking into jowls. She has thought about leaving him, of course, but what about the children? They love their father, and she knows he would fight to get custody. A corporate lawyer against a neurotic, panic-attack-afflicted middle-aged woman? No contest.

Without warning, the cat from earlier appears at her feet and she jumps, causing Henry to wake up. The night is fully dark now, but the cat's white fur is illuminated by the patio light. It winds its way around Tessa's legs, and she is quick to brush it away. It jumps up onto the rattan coffee table, and Amelia laughs and starts taking photos with her phone. The cat twirls and pirouettes.

'That's it!' Alistair is laughing, too. 'Time for bed.' He claps his hands and shoos the cat off the table and it makes for the bushes that surround the villa. Amelia tries to argue but eventually concedes and deposits her phone on the table. Henry, by now, has his thumb back in his mouth and is standing, tired and sullen.

'I'll be up in a minute,' says Alistair, as the children kiss Tessa on the cheek and say goodnight. She hugs Amelia, but when it is Henry's turn she pulls him in even closer, relishing the warmth of his little body against hers. She knows it is wrong to have a favourite, but she can't help it. Even at the age of seven, he is still her baby. Sometimes, after a panic attack, when she is recovering in bed, the anxiety forces her to skirt around her worst fear. She can't even bear to think about it.

When Alistair comes back down after tucking the children in he pours himself a large whisky and resumes his place in the rattan armchair. He picks up the leaflets again.

'This sounds good,' he says, without looking up. He brandishes a leaflet in her general direction and reads out loud. '"Timanfaya National Park is made up entirely of volcanic soil. Even though the volcano now lies dormant, temperatures of up to 270°C have been recorded at a depth of just ten centimetres and it is possible to feel the infernal heat of the earth's core right beneath your feet."' He takes a swig of whisky.

'"Come and feel the heat of the caldera – the cauldron – the crater formed by the island's last volcanic eruption in the eighteenth century. Lanzarote's dry climate means that the volcanic landscape is relatively unchanged since that time."' He looks up at her.

'I reckon we should go tomorrow. Have a lazy morning and then take a drive. We'll have to get a coach into the park itself, but the children will enjoy it.'

'Yes, if you like.' She reaches forward and takes the leaflet from where Alistair has replaced it on the coffee table. It depicts the same landscape she saw from the plane, barren and dismal, with an incongruous coachload of smiling tourists superimposed onto it. Alongside sits a crudely-depicted representation of a devil, with splayed limbs and curved horns and brandishing a five-pronged pitchfork above its head. A forked tail hangs down obscenely between its legs. It is grinning.

'What's that?' she asks her husband.

He barely glances up from the next leaflet he is reading. 'It's the logo. The logo for the national park. They call it the Timanfaya Devil.'

Tessa traces her finger over the dark red devil and suddenly the night is a little chillier. She pulls her cardigan tighter around her shoulders. She picks up some of Alistair's discarded leaflets and gives them a cursory glance. They sit in silence for a few long minutes until Alistair feigns a yawn and stretches his hands above his head.

'That's me done in. Long day, and all that. I'm off to bed.'

She manages not to flinch as he kisses the top of her head. She knows she won't sleep just yet. She feels twitchy and alert, and she is aware that it is being in a new place that has done this. She always feels on edge when she is out of her routine, her natural environment. She picks up Amelia's phone and checks her emails. Just the usual vapid junk from her friends, and her Facebook and Instagram accounts yield nothing she has to worry about. Tessa opens the photo app, and the cat appears, stark against the dark night where the camera flash has bounced off its pale white fur. She scrolls through, each photo showing the cat in a slightly different pose, the night still dark behind it. She gets to the last photo and pauses.

The cat has vanished.

The darkness is still there, filling the screen, but in the top right-hand corner there is a face. It is a man's face and it appears white out of the blackness, like an X-ray. The man's head is thrown back and his eyes are wide. His mouth is open, and the feeling that comes over her is one of unspeakable anguish; he is in extreme pain. Her eyes flash upwards, to the space behind where the cat was standing, towards the burnt house, searching for an intruder. She starts to feel the welling up of terror in her chest, but she closes her eyes and breathes in deeply through her nose. The feeling subsides. She looks again at the darkness, towards the little house on the other side of the road. She can see nothing. She looks at the phone, and the screaming man's face is still there. She taps the dustbin icon and then *delete photo*. The image disappears. A digital blip, she tells herself, one photo overlaying another, a visual anomaly. But perhaps she will go to bed after all. She is shivering.

Sunlight is creeping around the bedroom blinds when she wakes. She listens for Alistair's breathing, but there is nothing, so she rolls over and sees that he has gone. She looks at her phone. Nearly eight o'clock; it isn't like her to sleep so late.

She's halfway down the stairs when she hears the knocking. The man at the front door is dark and slight, with a generous moustache that curls over his top lip. Her first thought is that he looks worried.

'*Disculpe.*' He turns and raises a hand in the direction of the burnt-out house behind him. '*He venido a—*'

She raises her hand, the palm flat and towards him. 'I'm sorry. I'll get my husband. He speaks Spanish.' She leaves him standing at the door and calls to Alistair. He comes in from the kitchen, wiping his hands on a tea towel.

Alistair begins a rapid and fluid conversation with the man.

The man is holding out his hands, apologetically, and Alistair is frowning, then nodding. Tessa is able to pick out a few individual words – *sí, problema, entiendo* – but the rest is just a torrent of consonants and vowels. As she listens, however, her ears settle into the rhythm of the language, and she finds she can pick out other individual words – *desafortunado, maldito* – words that are in themselves meaningless, but when combined with the scorched shell of the house, take on a more meaningful intensity.

Eventually Alistair shakes hands with the man. He closes the door behind him and runs a hand through his hair.

'What's the matter?' Tessa asks.

'Nothing. It's nothing, really. Nothing to worry about, anyway. He just came to say that they were going to start demolishing the house over the road, and to apologise for the noise.'

'The burnt house? The one that's all boarded up?'

'Yes, apparently it's structurally unsound. It can't be restored, so the owner has asked him – he's the builder – to demolish it and rebuild it from scratch.'

'Seems rather extreme. It didn't look that badly damaged.'

Alistair shrugs. 'Probably an insurance job. Anyway, there's no point us hanging around here today. The noise is going to be unbearable. Shall we drive up to the national park and get on a coach?'

Tessa thinks about the desolate landscape, the black volcanic rock and the giant, empty crater. And then she thinks about the photo of the screaming man and the burnt-out house just over the road.

'Yes. Yes, why not?'

The Devil of Timanfaya

*

There are no signs of life at all, she thinks, just rocks and dust and ash. This is what it must be like to be on the moon. From where the coach is parked she can see down into the caldera – the cauldron – and the huge crater does indeed look as though a giant hand has scooped out the earth to create an enormous cooking pot. The insides are incinerated, scorched; nothing grows there.

The coach starts up again and jagged banks of black rock soar on either side. As it progresses along the road she can see that a few meagre paths have been forged, each about a foot wide and covered in a fine dust that has resulted from the passage of hikers. The rest of the landscape is littered with craggy boulders and is untraversable, and her mind settles on the thought that no human being has ever walked there. Here, inland, the clouds have settled, the translucent blue sky that met them at the airport yesterday has become mottled and overcast, as though that unseen hand has drawn a veil over it. She shakes her head, as if that will dispel these peculiar thoughts.

Slouched next to her, Amelia is not looking out of the window; her attention is given solely to her phone. Alistair turns round from the seat in front of them which he shares with Henry. He gives her an overly-cheerful smile.

'OK?'

She knows he is being considerate, but his attentiveness grates. It's been months since she had a panic attack, but he always seems to walk on eggshells around her. Sometimes she feels like an Edwardian lady, given to bouts of hysteria.

'I'm fine, honestly.'

The coach pulls up at a brick building – the visitors' centre – and the tour guide speaks over the tannoy, telling them that they are about to witness a geothermal experiment that will demonstrate the intense heat that lies just below the surface. They alight from the coach and Tessa takes hold of Henry's hand. It is comfortable: warm and soft. As they make their way across the black path, he stops, and stands stock still. His grip on her hand becomes tighter.

'Henry? What is it?'

He points to the sign at the front of the visitors' centre. It is a primitive construction made of metal and two horizontal planks of wood. Standing on the bottom plank is an iron depiction of the Timanfaya Devil, its legs crudely splayed. It is holding aloft another piece of timber, and across both pieces of wood the words *Parque Nacional Timanfaya* are written in rusty orange text. The devil's spiked tail hangs lewdly between its legs, pointing down, into the ground, into the bowels of the earth. The iron from which its face has been forged has rusted away, and the mouth has spread upwards; on one side it touches its ear.

She turns Henry away from the sign and pulls him towards her. She tells him it is just a picture, it's nothing to worry about. He's still glancing at the devil and biting his bottom lip when they catch up with the rest of the group. They join the throng of tourists being ushered towards a clearing to the side of the building and find themselves standing in a ring around a man holding a bucket. He is a little, brown-skinned wizened old man, not unlike the builder from that morning. The tour guide explains that there is a crack in the earth's crust which allows a direct passage down to the molten lava below. The man proceeds to pour water into the hole, and jumps backwards, just as a huge plume of steam gushes up.

The tour guide beams. 'See? Here we prove that the earth still burns.'

Tessa watches in silence. When the display finishes she turns to give the sign one last look. The devil grins back.

The coach takes them back to the base of the national park, and the four of them disembark and make their way to the hire car. Amelia is walking and looking at her phone at the same time, oblivious to everything around her. Henry lags behind, using his foot to draw shapes in the black dust that covers the ground, and Tessa turns to tell him to hurry up. This is when she sees the man. He is standing on the other side of the car park, leaning on a stone wall. Despite the heat he is wearing a black hoodie, the hood pulled up, and black jeans. Slouching, he has his hands in his pockets. He is looking away from her, and she can't see his face, but she can tell that he is watching Henry.

'Come along, Henry.' She runs to him and grabs his wrist and drags him to the car. The man is now looking at his feet, kicking at the dirt, and she still can't see his face.

Their return to the villa is met with noise and dust from the house on the other side of the road. The little man from that morning is standing by the house, directing a lorry as it reverses onto the road. When he sees their car he holds up a hand to the truck driver to stop and allow them to pass.

They alight from the car and she ushers the children across the patio area and towards the house. Alistair stands outside for a while and watches the commotion over the road. When he joins her in the kitchen he is preoccupied and quiet and doesn't respond to her suggestion of a barbeque for dinner. Then he nods to himself, decisive.

'Let's go out, eh?'

That night, she dreams of the Timanfaya Devil. She is at the caldera, the visitors' centre, and she is leaning over the crack in the ground where the man had poured the water. The earth peels apart before her and clawed hands appear. They grip onto the riven earth at each side and a creature emerges, head first. It is wearing the black hoodie of the man from the car park. It pulls itself from the earth and reveals four splayed limbs, and a long, curling, forked tail. It lifts its head to her and she sees that it has the white face of the man in the photo. The sinews in its neck become taut, straining, as the head is pulled backwards. What remains of the flesh around the mouth is stretched tight over blackened teeth, and the gaping hole reaches up to its ears. It screams, an anguished, piercing sound that speaks of all the pain in hell.

Then it is down on all fours, and it scuttles towards her.

She turns and runs, but the black dust is slippery beneath her feet and she slips. She pushes herself up and thrusts herself forward along the path, and even without looking, she knows that the creature is scampering after her. She can hear its hooves scraping on the volcanic soil; it is gaining on her. She runs along the hikers' path for what seems like an eternity, and then she is suddenly outside the burnt-out house, except it is not burnt now; it is a pristine white and the windows are intact. She pushes open the front door, knowing that the devil is at her heels. She slams the door behind her and runs into the house. She runs from room to room, and they are the rooms in her house at home, the living room and the kitchen and her bedroom, and they are familiar, but not quite right. The furniture has been moved, has been rearranged, and it stands in front of the windows, blocking her escape. Then comes the smell, the acrid reek of smoke, and when she turns to retrace her steps, she sees the flames licking down the hallway towards her. She is screaming, begging the devil to let her out, when she wakes.

She checks her phone, which is charging on the bedside table. It is almost morning, and she knows she won't be able to get back to sleep, so she creeps downstairs and makes a cup of tea. Amelia's phone is on the kitchen counter and she picks it up. Before she knows what she is doing, she has the Safari app open and she is googling the name of their street, and she tries to remember some of the Spanish words she heard Alistair using with the builder. There are no meaningful results, so she tries again, in English this time: the name of the street and *house, fire, burn*.

The first result is an article from the *Daily Express* from six weeks ago. All her search terms are there, and there is even a photograph of the house. She steels herself to read the article. A child abducted – a ten-year-old English boy on holiday with his parents – and imprisoned in the little house. The house was identified by vigilantes as the hideout of the perpetrator and they rescued the boy, who escaped unharmed. They then locked the abductor in the house and set it on fire. He burned alive.

Tessa feels the first prickling of anxiety, and puts the phone down before she drops it. She recognises the symptoms, and that in itself is something. She can feel the breath leaving her body, her lungs struggling to cope with the lack of oxygen. She feels the usual difficulty in breathing, and she forces herself to take deep breaths, inhaling slowly and exhaling quickly. She can fight the dizziness; she knows that will be over soon. But what she struggles with is the feeling of dread, that insurmountable terror. The knowledge – and it is a knowledge, rather than a fear – that she will definitely die. It is something visceral, something tangible and real, and she knows it is only a matter of time and she surrenders herself to that knowledge.

She has no idea how long it is before she is conscious of herself again. She finds herself alone, shivering, leaning against the kitchen counter. Eventually her heart rate steadies, and her breathing becomes shallower and less urgent.

So this horror is what Alistair had been discussing with the builder. That was why the house had to be demolished.

The children are playing on the beach. She hasn't told Alistair about the newspaper article, or about the panic attack; he'd only worry and cosset her more. She has tried to push from her mind the potential fate of the child, but she finds herself clinging to the actual fate of the man. She tries vicariously to feel his pain, to feel how he felt as the fire consumed him. Her desire is at odds with the pleasant beach upon which she sits, and the joyful splashing of Amelia and Henry. Even as she thinks of the abductor's flesh melting, his skin glistening with burns as the fire takes him, she is conscious of her children playing in the surf.

Alistair is asleep on his beach towel, head tucked into chest, snoring gently.

'Mummy, can we have an ice cream?' Henry is before her, wet and encrusted in black sand, and she uses the palm of her hand to brush it from his legs and his arms.

'There isn't an ice-cream shop,' she says, still brushing.

'There is,' he says, and puts out his still-chubby arm to gesture in the direction of the headland. She looks to where he is pointing, and he's right: there's a little kiosk with red and yellow bunting on the other side of a long, low building she thinks must be a café or a restaurant.

'Alistair, can you keep an eye on them while I get us some ice creams?' Her husband's belly is already starting to redden. He lifts his head and shades his eyes with his hand.

'Vanilla for me,' he says, and sits up, resting himself on one elbow.

Tessa takes her purse from her bag and slides her feet into her sandals. The sand in them feels grainy and rough. Walking backwards up the beach, she sees that Henry has started to build a black sandcastle, and Amelia is still splashing in the shallows.

She reaches the road that runs alongside the beach and walks along the pavement until she comes to a café. She has to pass behind the building in order to reach the ice-cream kiosk, and as she does so, her view of the children is obscured. She finds herself hurrying, desperate to have them in her vision, and when she reaches the kiosk and can see them again, consumed in their activities, she lets out her breath and smiles at her own stupidity.

The transaction with the man behind the counter is performed and she balances the three ice creams in one hand, her other hand holding on to her purse. Then she looks back to where her children are on the beach. Amelia is sitting on a towel, her headphones in her ears, eyes on her phone screen.

Henry has abandoned his sandcastle and is standing, erect and rigid, staring out to sea.

Behind him stands the man. It is the man from the caldera, the man in the black hoodie.

She wants to scream, but she has no breath in her lungs. She looks for Alistair, and he is lying down, recumbent on the towel. Asleep.

She wants to run to her child, but if she does she will have to pass behind the café, which will obscure her view. What will she see when she gets to the other side? Part of her thinks that if she can keep her gaze on her son, she can protect him, but she can feel the constriction of her throat and her lungs. She knows that this time she will not survive the terror.

She watches in silence as the man raises his hand and places it on Henry's shoulder. Her son does not flinch. The man turns his head towards her, and as he peels back his hood she sees the terrible white face from the phone, from her dream, but now it is pitted and scorched, the flesh bubbling and wet. Just before the black tunnel closes around her she sees that the man's mouth is still open, even though the lips have been burnt away, but the man is not screaming. Now he is laughing.

Wretched

It's the growling in my stomach that makes my finger twitch on the trigger. I steady myself and readjust the angle of the tripod. The screen shows three of them, standing in a huddle. They're garbed in the semi-official uniform of the Wretched: filthy anoraks over woollen sweaters and tatty jeans, and each one is holding a lumpen bundle of bedding and possessions. I zoom in on the one on the left first: male, white. A beanie hat pulled down low over his forehead and an unkempt beard make it difficult to ascertain his age, but that's not my job. The red dot appears on my screen, and I swipe my finger and thumb across the touchpad to enlarge it, so that the whole of his face is covered by a pulsing circle.

I'm about to pull the trigger when he jerks his head to the side, and I have to readjust the bloody laser again. From the camera's vantage point on the second floor of the multi-storey car park I have a sweeping view across the ring road and down to the canal. It's late in the afternoon, and the concrete walls of the flyover merge with the sky.

I'm distracted, and I force myself to refocus the sight on the Wretched. Once I am sure he's not going to make any sudden movements, I squeeze. On my screen, his image is frozen, caught in the red circle. I quickly move the sight to the other two and *bam, bam*, pick them off in quick succession. I double click on the touchpad and then hit *transmit*.

When I get home, I'm surprised to see that Cassie is up and about and has already made a start on dinner. She's standing at the sink, but she doesn't turn around when I open the door, even though, from the way her back stiffens, I know she's heard me. I stand for a moment, drinking her in. She's thinner than ever, and her shoulder blades point at me, sharp, through her thin cardigan.

There is protein frying on the hob. It's the usual smell: sweet, but with something sharp that clings to the back of the throat. They say it's from hanging it – like they do with beef – to tenderise it and make it more palatable. It took me a while to get my head around the idea of eating it, and at first Cassie refused to touch it. She said she'd decided to go vegetarian, and I'd gone along with it, and watched her getting thinner and thinner. She'd tried to grow vegetables on the windowsill of the flat, but there wasn't enough natural light and the seeds hadn't even sprouted. After a couple of months she'd had to start eating the stuff or she would have starved, just like her sister. Sometimes, there's only so far your principles will get you.

Finally, she turns around and acknowledges me with a nod. Her skin is sallow and greasy, and pimples are sprouting on her forehead and chin. I get that pain in my chest when I see how sharp her cheekbones are, how hollow her eye sockets have become. She's still beautiful, though.

'How was work?' she asks, and I shrug.

'Fine,' I say. 'I got three targets, so that's good.' She winces and looks away. I go over and put a hand round her, and when it settles on her back I can count the notches of her spine with my fingers. She looks up at me, and all of a sudden I'm pleading with her.

'We need money to eat, Cass. Look at you. You're wasting away.' I notice that her hair is thinner, and there's the first sign of a bald patch on one temple. She sees me looking and puts up a hand to cover it. The movement is frail and childlike and I feel myself crumbling. 'It's not like I'm hurting them, Cass.' I'm begging now. 'I'm not the one rounding them up. I'm just collecting their data for the cops. They're the ones doing the bad stuff.'

She turns back to the sink and neither of us speaks for several minutes. I lay the table and slice the cooked protein. It oozes blood onto the chopping board: paler than beef, darker than pork. Cassie pours two glasses of water from the tap. I haven't eaten yet today and, despite myself, my mouth is watering, and there is an acute tension in the underside of my jaw. We sit in silence and stare at our plates, hers with barely a few slices, mine with more.

'Bon appétit,' I say, in an attempt to lighten the mood. She keeps her eyes on her plate and stabs. Raises the fork to her mouth and chews, hard. The tendons in her neck stick out like ropes.

*

The next day is a Sunday – my day off – and I get up early and walk along the canal into town. Even though there's a fair wind, the sky is overcast and the stagnant water throws back flat, grey cloud. The towpath used to be a hotbed for the Wretched, but they seem to have moved on in the last few weeks, since the crackdown. In all honesty, it's unusual to see them out in daylight these days, so I'm feeling pretty smug about the ones I bagged yesterday.

My walk takes me past the Waitrose on Commercial Street, but the barriers are still up after the raids last week, and there are armed guards at either side of the entrance, their machine guns slung across their chests like monstrous musical instruments. I keep my head down and try not to make eye contact.

I cross the river over the old bridge and there's Giggsy, standing outside the Bull and Flag, his dented mountain bike propped against the pebble-dashed wall. He gives me a grin, all brown teeth and cold sores.

'Alright, mate?' His voice is nasal and there's a trail of slime running down his upper lip. He must see me looking because he swipes at it with the back of his hand.

Giggsy's got a mate who works at the Waitrose. Not a fluffer or a shuffler or anything fancy like that. He's a van man, and so he's not meant to have access to the produce, but he's found a way of pilfering items from the pallets as they're unloading and he, in turn, unloads them onto Giggsy.

'What have you got, then, eh?' I'm trying to act cool, but really I'm shitting myself; I could go straight back inside for breaching my parole like this. Giggsy lets out a little high-pitched giggle.

'I-got-cake-I-got-cheese-I-got-bro-cco-li.' He sings this, rather than saying it, and I know he's taking the piss.

'How much?' I ask.

'Fifty for the lot,' he says, in his whiny voice, and he takes a rollie from behind his ear and puts it in his mouth.

'Christ, mate, that's a bit steep isn't it?'

He takes the rollie back out of his mouth and jabs it in the air at me. 'If you want it, you pay, alright? Simple as. I got other customers, you know.'

I take out my wallet and turn around so he can't see as I peel off two twenties and a tenner. I got paid last night at the end of my shift and there's a fold of notes in there but it's not enough, not really, not if we're going to make up the rent this week. I hand over the money. Giggsy picks up the knapsack that's slung over the handlebars of his bike and hands me a paper bag from it. It's a lot smaller than I was expecting. He knows what I'm thinking, because he swings one leg over the bike and pushes himself off. He sets off over the bridge, and I think I can hear him shout, 'Loser,' but I can't be sure, as it's lost on the wind.

I hide the bag under my coat and head back towards home, looking forward to showing my loot to Cassie. I stop to turn up my collar against the wind and realise that I'm opposite the Waitrose. I risk a glance up. There's a woman in a designer jacket and high heels, her hair piled up in a manner even I know to be expensive. I guess that on the Value Index she'd be somewhere around a B65 or a C70. It's a game Cassie and I play – or used to play – whenever we were out: to try to guess from someone's appearance where they score on the Val-In.

From a patent leather handbag the woman takes out a purse, and from that she removes a card. The guard takes one hand off his machine gun and inspects the card closely. It's not quite the level of scrutiny you get at passport control, but it's still fairly rigorous. He even lets go of the machine gun, allowing it to hang from the strap around his shoulder, and uses a finger to rub at the surface of the card, making sure it's not a forgery. Finally, he takes a hand scanner from his back pocket and points it at the card, then he angles the scanner at the woman's face. She lifts her chin and looks straight ahead. He looks at the screen on the scanner and then nods and the woman walks into the store. Before she moves out of sight, I see her stoop to pick up a basket. The guard resumes his position, the machine gun hoisted across his midriff, and I'm aware of the rustling of the paper bag under my jacket as I turn onto the towpath.

The canal hasn't been used in years, and the water is still and oily and home only to empty drinks cans and bags for life. There's a billboard high up on the side of an old factory on the other side. It's just one massive Union Jack, with a single sentence superimposed in stark black text:

MAKING OUR STREETS SAFE AGAIN.

It's ironic, really. That's the government's latest slogan, but hardly anyone risks going out at night these days, unless it's to do bad stuff or to go to work. They can say anything they like, though: all the billboards are owned by one company now. It happened fairly quickly. One firm bought out all its competitors, or forced them out of the market, and just kept expanding, while reinforcing the government message. Cassie said it was like a vaccine: by dripping miniscule amounts of poison into the public's consciousness via the billboards, society was being immunised against the realisation of what the government was doing. The same company that owns the billboards was also given the contracts to run the trains and the prisons, and then the hospitals.

I'm halfway along the towpath when I spot a pack of about a dozen masks twenty metres or so ahead. They're standing at the entrance to a building site, waiting for the foreman to arrive, I guess. I wonder about turning back and going the long way round, past the multistorey, but they seem more afraid of me that I am of them, and they shrink back as I approach. I stop and take a good look at them, each one indistinguishable from the next, other than in height and build: black jeans, black hoodies, and a grey, moulded-plastic face mask. The only thing that sets them apart from one another are the QR codes tattooed on the backs of their hands, and even they all look the same to the untrained eye.

The general election had resulted in another landslide, and it wasn't long after that the first steps were taken towards the Initiative. Of course, no-one knew what it was all about then. There was a big publicity campaign, inviting people to come forward to have their faces mapped by computers, and a 3D model was produced which, the company behind it announced, was the representation of the aggregated features of the volunteers – a literal portrait of British society. At first, it was claimed, an enormous sculpture would be produced – *The Face of Britain* – which would be displayed on the fourth plinth at Trafalgar Square, a kind of coming-together of all the different people who make up British society, a celebration of diversity. When this failed to materialise, the delays were put down to technical issues to do with the sculpting process, and then it was reported that some of the people involved had changed their minds about having their faces used in this way. One of the anti-government websites stuck its neck out and claimed that the data was being used to produce visors: twelve thousand identical grey moulded-plastic face shields. At the time this was neither confirmed nor denied, but not long afterwards the masks started to appear on the streets.

They're cowering away from me now, shrinking into the chain-link fence, and not for the first time I wonder if the rumours about what has been done to their faces are true.

When I get back Cassie is in bed, the curtains still closed, even though it's eleven o'clock. There's a pale light filtering through the thin curtains and it renders her fragile and vulnerable, like a fledgling abandoned in a nest. I stand there, just watching her for a moment. She moves her legs under the covers and groans. I draw back the curtains and she rolls over, away from me.

'Look, Cass, look what I got us.' It's the rustle of the paper bag that makes her turn back round, and she opens her eyes and allows herself a smile when I empty the bag onto the bed and she sees the yellowing broccoli, the stale cake, the rubbery cheese. She reaches out and touches the bag, and then she places her hand on the back of mine and I know it's going to be alright.

When Cassie and I first got together I'd just been let out of prison. I'd been dumped, along with a dozen other ex-cons, under the railway arches, with just a sleeping bag and a couple of quid. A few of the others knew of an illicit charity that worked out of an empty shop on the ring road and ran a foodbank, and I tagged along with them. Cassie was volunteering there and we got chatting. She wasn't that friendly at first, and kept herself to herself unless she had to organise the other volunteers or talk to customers: she'd stand at the back of the shop with a couple of the other helpers – a tall, bearded guy called Gav and a small, dumpy woman they just called AJ – and they'd be whispering furiously, or showing each other stuff on their phones. I started calling in every day just to see her, and eventually, when she did look up, she'd acknowledge me with a nod, and then a smile. Gav would give me the evils, though, and it was obvious that he fancied her. With hindsight, I think it was the threat of competition from Gav that made me ask Cassie out so quickly, but even then it took a few weeks to persuade her to go for a coffee with me.

We'd agreed to meet at a café on the High Street. It was one of those perfect summer's days, the sky a brilliant, cloudless blue and the heat from the sun gentle and welcome, rather than harsh and oppressive. We sat at a table on the pavement and ordered iced coffees. I remember how Cassie wouldn't quite look at me at first; she just swirled her drink, looking down at the table, smiling. That was when I noticed the tattoo on her inner forearm, up near her elbow. It looked like the outline of a wave, a curve that rose up and curled over itself before flattening out again. It reminded me of a poster one of my cellmates used to have – a famous Japanese woodcutting he'd said, and he'd told me the artist's name, but I'd forgotten it. I was going to mention this to Cassie, and ask her about her tattoo, but she looked up and saw me staring. She pulled her sleeve down to cover it and went back to stirring her coffee.

I realised then that she was actually quite shy, that the person she was at the food bank – organising and instructing people, advising and directing – wasn't really her. There was a softness to her, an ethereal, waif-like quality that was at odds with the blurred, dark blue ink of the tattoo. It seemed incongruous – violent, even – against the faintly translucent flesh of her forearm.

'What was it like inside?' Her question surprised me. We'd been making small talk up until then – discussing our families and where we'd grown up – and it took me a couple of seconds to answer her.

'Not bad, I suppose,' I said eventually. 'Could have been worse. I just kept my head down and got on with it. As long as you don't get yourself into trouble, the time passes soon enough.' She nodded and went back to stirring her coffee.

'What were you in for?'

'Just a couple of bits of joyriding, graffiti, that sort of thing. It just all added up, and the last time was the straw that broke the camel's back, I guess. I got six months.' She nodded again, as though she was satisfied with the answer.

'What about you?' I asked. 'What do you do when you're not at the food bank?' She looked around her, at the other customers and the waitress and down at the pavement, as if she was trying to decide what to say. After a few moments, she looked back at me and opened her mouth to speak, but then, all of a sudden, she was grinning and looking over my shoulder. I turned to see that a tiny bird had landed on the back of the spare chair next to me, just a couple of feet away. Small and brown, it had flashes of paler brown on its wings and around its eyes. Cassie was beaming.

'A wren,' she said. 'I haven't seen one of those since I was a kid.' She was the happiest I'd seen anyone look in ages; her whole face had lit up, and her pleasure was contagious. I found myself laughing, and then she started, too. The bird looked at us as if we were nuts and flew off, but it had sparked something.

On Monday I'm on the late shift. Before I leave, I make Cassie a cup of tea and I've got the radio on because sometimes the silence of the flat is too much. She's having a lie down, which I know will merge with bedtime and she'll just doze on and off until I get back tomorrow. Something comes on the radio about a 25 per cent reduction in the number of Wretched, and a corresponding increase in the number of Treated (the official term for masks). They interview the Social and Moral Justice Minister, who says that if it continues along these lines, the country will have eradicated the Wretched by 2030. Then someone from the opposition comes on, but they aren't really given a chance to respond. They just about manage to mention the escapes from the treatment centres, and the four Interims that are on the run, before the presenter cuts them off.

Cassie's asleep when I take in her tea, so I leave it on the nightstand with the last chunk of cake and give her a kiss on the forehead. There's a sheen of sweat there and she feels hot. I double lock the door on my way out.

*

After that first date at the café, Cassie and I started spending more time together. Nothing fancy, just a walk in the park, or meeting for a coffee. I suggested that maybe I should volunteer at the food bank, so we could see more of each other, but she didn't seem keen, and said I should concentrate on getting a paying job. Gav still looked daggers at me whenever I called in to walk Cassie home after she'd finished her shift, and even though she never said anything, I got the impression they might have had history. He always tried to act the hard man around me, puffing his chest out and pushing his shoulders back, all textbook tough guy stuff. It amused me, really – I think he felt threatened by my ex-con status. One afternoon, when Cassie was late because she was drawing up the inventory, Gav came out and did the classic thing of rolling up his shirt sleeves when he saw me, and that's when I saw his tattoo: a dark blue wave shape, curving up and over. The same design as Cassie's.

After we'd been seeing each other for about six months, she asked me to move into her flat, and we had a bit of a celebration. Our Value Index had gone from an H12 (me: ex-con) and an E25 (Cassie: graduate, good employment prospects) to a collective E37 (part of the Val-In was aggregated for a couple who were co-habiting; the government thought it increased stability which led to greater productivity and thus value). We took our newly issued Val-In card and spent a small fortune – by our standards – in the Tesco on the ring road, and gorged ourselves on fresh fruit and vegetables until there was juice running down our chins and our bellies were straining. I remember thinking at the time that it was Cassie who had got me here. She saved me. I was a hair's breadth from being like all the other ex-cons. Wretched.

At weekends, we'd go on protests together. It wasn't hardcore stuff, and certainly nothing illegal: the conditions of my parole meant I'd be chucked back inside straight away if I put a foot wrong. It was just waving placards as we wandered up and down the High Street along with Cassie's mates, or writing letters to our MP asking awkward questions about government policy – which were never answered. It wasn't much, but it was something, and we needed to feel that we were fighting back. Cassie, in particular, would get really angry that not enough people were doing anything. She said it was as though a collective apathy had blanketed the country, like a layer of ash had been deposited on everyone from a previously extinct volcano and rendered everyone immobile. Fossilised indifference, she called it.

A woman from the agency called on a Friday morning while Cassie was at the food bank. They had a job for me. She described the setup at the flat, said that training would be provided to use the gear, and mentioned a wage that was peanuts. I knew immediately that Cassie would hate it, of course, and so I tried to tell the woman that I'd wait to see what else came along. She reminded me in a bored voice that accepting the first job I was offered, no matter what, was one of the conditions of my parole. Shit.

I met Cassie at work that afternoon and suggested a walk in the park; I didn't want to be confined to the flat when I told her about the job. It was one of those overcast winter's days, with the branches hanging low and leafless and a dampness in the air that wasn't rain, but would still saturate your clothes and your hair. Cassie had on a long, thick woollen coat and a huge, grey knitted scarf, and she looked tiny and vulnerable in the enormous layers. I waited until we were standing at the duck pond, her favourite place in the park, even though there were no ducks left there anymore. The water was clouded with the green scum of algae.

At first she looked incredulous when I told her, and then she went ballistic.

'For fuck's sake. You'll be a part of the Initiative, don't you see? You'll be one of them.' She started pacing up and down the edge of the pond, hands clenched and eyes flashing. I was terrified she was going to dump me, ask me to move out. I'd been worrying about it all day.

'It's not my fault.' I started to recite the speech I'd prepared, even though I knew it sounded weak, pathetic. 'I have to take it or—'

'Yes, I know, they'll chuck you back inside,' she shouted. She stopped walking and turned away to stare out over the pond. The light was starting to fade by then and the water was flat and blank, reflecting an empty sky. She stood there for ages, completely still, and then after a while her shoulders started to shake. When she turned around, her eyes were wet. 'Well, I suppose we have no choice. You'll have to take it.' There was a bitterness in her voice I hadn't heard before, even when she was on one of her rants. I reached out to her, tried to put my hand on her shoulder, but she pushed me away and ran off. I considered following her, then thought it was best if I left her to calm down.

I walked back to the flat along the High Street, conscious that it was almost dark and that Cassie was out on her own. By the time I got home I'd phoned her half a dozen times, and each time it had gone straight to voicemail. I hung my coat up and fried up some protein and ate it leaning against the kitchen worktop, feeling my jaw working mechanically against the spongy resistance. There was a bottle of tequila on top of the fridge that I'd got off Giggsy and we were saving for a special occasion, but I felt suddenly reckless and unscrewed the cap and downed a mouthful, and then another. Fuck her, I thought. It wasn't my fault. I had no choice in the matter: I had to take the job. Anyway, I didn't need to worry about Cassie – she'd be out with her mates from the food bank: fat AJ and that lanky twat Gav. Gav with the tattoo.

I grabbed a tumbler from the draining board and half filled it with tequila, then I sat at the kitchen table and picked up my phone. I didn't mean to snoop on her. I'd asked her a couple of times about her tattoo, but she'd always change the subject, fob me off. I'd never really pushed it, always felt that if she wanted to tell me she would. Now felt like a good time to do some research.

I spent a couple of hours on a reverse image search, drilling down through the vestiges of defunct websites, following dead links and getting lost down worm holes, all the time with half an eye out for a notification to tell me that Cassie had messaged me. By the time I found something, my eyes were raw and the tequila bottle was half empty.

It was a pretty inconclusive result, even I had to admit. It was a news site that hadn't been updated for a year or so, which seemed to consist mainly of articles about activists and what they'd done – a sort of fan club for anti-government disruptors. There was one article about the Reprieve hack, which rang a faint bell, and as I read on I found out why. When I was inside a group had hacked into the systems at the Ministry for Social and Moral Justice and taken down their databases, resulting in thousands of prisoners' records being wiped. It had been all that anyone had spoken about for weeks, all the cons wondering if their criminal records had been destroyed. The news site claimed that a group called Insurgency was behind the hack, but gave very little information about the group itself. It said that their main objective had been to disrupt the government's tech: hack into websites, force databases to crash, basically anything that would enable 'a tidal wave to rise up against the threat to democracy'. Its logo was a wave.

It was the snick of the front door closing that woke me. I was still sitting at the kitchen table, slumped forward, my neck twisted at an awkward angle, and I only just managed to sit upright when Cassie walked into the living room. My head felt heavy and sodden, and I couldn't remember if I should be angry or compliant. I decided the best policy was to let Cassie speak first.

She'd taken her coat and scarf off and looked fragile in her leggings and enormous boots. Her mascara was halfway down her cheeks. She didn't say anything for ages, and then she came over and slid onto my lap. I pushed the chair back from the table to make more room and she wrapped her arms around my neck and pushed her chin in under my ear.

'I'm sorry,' she said. 'I know it's not your fault.'

I ran a hand through my hair and could feel how much I was sweating.

'I'm glad you're home,' I said. 'I was worried about you.'

'I'm fine. I went to AJ's.' She sniffed. 'Have you been drinking?'

'Yeah, sorry. I fucked up.'

She smiled. 'It's OK. I never really liked tequila much, anyway.' She brought her arms back round and laid her hands in her lap. Her sleeve had ridden up and her tattoo was just visible, peeking out from the edge of the fabric. I reached out and touched it with the back of my finger, just lightly, a moth's touch. She flinched, and frowned slightly, but she didn't say anything or pull away.

Nothing else was mentioned about the argument, that night or the next day. There was a truce, an unspoken agreement. In fact, the only trace of it ever having happened was my blistering hangover.

A few months after that evening Cassie got ill and had to stop working at the food bank, and quickly went downhill, day after day. Eventually, she couldn't leave the house and had to stop going out to meet her mates as well. The first thing we knew about being downgraded to a G15 on the Val-In was when the new card arrived in the post, along with directions to the processing centre and instructions for downloading the Protein Voucher app.

There's a café over the road from the tower block where the control room is, and if I'm on the late shift I always go there first and make my cup of tea last an hour. That way, I've done the walk through town while it's still light, and it's just a quick dash across the estate in time to start work. It's the usual guy behind the counter, and even though we've never made conversation, he'll start to pour the cuppa when he sees me come in. He seems nervous tonight, and his eyes keep flitting behind me to the door.

I'm blowing the steam off the top of my tea when my phone buzzes. It's Kenny, my supervisor.

LADS. TRIPLE PAY FOR ANYONE WHO NABS ONE OF THEM INTERIMS TONIGHT. GO FOR THE QR.

I sit up straight in my chair. I think of the vegetables and fruit I could buy for Cassie. Salad, even, and milk. If I was careful and didn't have any myself, she wouldn't have to eat protein for weeks. She might even get well again.

Some days, I find it difficult to remember what it was like before the Initiative was introduced. It seemed to come in gradually, the country being drip-fed new information in the weeks and months after the election. The first real sign of it was the early release of prisoners with less than a year to go on their sentences, in a bid, the government said, to ease over-crowding. No-one seemed to be concerned about why so many ex-cons were let out all at once, at least not until it transpired that there were no support systems in place and they were just being dumped on the streets.

As crime levels rose, so did the country's indignation. Some places adopted semi-official curfews, and for a while there was wide-scale moral outrage. Eyebrows were raised in the press when the company that ran the prisons was given the job of turning the empty ones into treatment centres, but that, like everything else, didn't last long and was quickly subsumed into the national consciousness. And then there were the rumours, of course, about what went on in these places.

One of the left-wing websites published an exposé, alleging that there was intelligence profiling, with those at the higher end of the scale immediately deemed unsuitable for treatment; they would be sent directly to the processing centres. It was claimed that the Interims were dealt with in an appallingly demeaning fashion in order to break their will, in much the same way as wild horses would be 'broken' to make them more pliable: they needed to be made suitable for institutionalised work after they were released. There were rumours about what was done to them physically, to dehumanise them, but even the left-wing outlets wouldn't report on that.

The control room is in a flat in a derelict tower block next to the ring road. After I'd come to terms with the fact I had to take the job, I allowed myself to entertain the idea that it might be interesting – exciting even – and I had visions of being given a night-scope camera and stalking my prey through all kinds of terrain, like a real-life assassin. Of course, I knew I'd never actually be killing anyone, and remembering these expectations makes me feel embarrassed as I let myself into the flat on the fourth floor. I'm sweating after walking up all the piss-stinking stairs because the piss-stinking lift doesn't work. My gear – a screen equipped with a laser sight and transmitter – is all set up in the bedroom of the flat. The bed is still there, a pink candlewick bedspread wrinkled over the surface. Not the hideout of a world-renowned assassin.

The camera I control is only half a mile away, but the signal from it is encrypted, and then bounced around the world, from one VPN to another, to make it more difficult for the sabs to intercept. On slow days, I like to imagine the footage ricocheting around the world, from one city to the next, before ending up here, in the control room, a blink of an eye later. I'm paid to sit on the bed (there's no chair) and just watch the screen until I see movement. The flat's been derelict for years and I open the window onto the tiny balcony to try to clear some of the smell. I settle down and wait.

I've been there for about twenty minutes, and I'm thinking about having a nap, when there's movement at the bottom left of the screen. I zoom the camera in using the touch pad, and the image on the screen is enlarged, but it turns out just to be a pair of cops. They're looking at their scanners, and I'm guessing they've just had a report of a sighting. They'll have access to a map, which will show the area in the immediate vicinity. Overlaid onto the map will be the locations of the Wretched that have just been sent in by people like me – people sat in grotty flats in derelict tower blocks all over the city, paid peanuts to monitor cameras and scan faces. The data we capture is logged onto the Initiative's main database and at the same time the facial recognition info is sent to the cops, along with the location of the Wretched. It's easy to round them up after that. Like shooting fish in a barrel.

The police move out of view of the camera, and I lie back on the bed, but it's only a matter of seconds before there's movement again, and a figure peels itself out of the shadows, as if it was waiting for the cops to go. It has the usual dark clothing and pale face of a mask, and I'm wondering whether to grass it up for being out after curfew when something makes me sit up. It's the face.

The face is not the grey moulded-plastic I've got used to seeing on the ones I've passed working on building sites or waiting to be let into factories. It's like flesh, but at the same time, it's not. I zoom the camera in and, on the screen, the face is suddenly magnified, massively enlarged, and my stomach heaves. There is no mask but it is no longer identifiable as an individual, or even as a human. And suddenly I realise that all the rumours about what goes on in the treatment centres are true. When some people said that the treatment involved cosmetic surgery to remove any identifying features from the faces of the Wretched, they were telling the truth. But it's worse than that. The eyes are merely two black holes in a flat space. Two nostrils remain but there is no nose, and it looks as though the lips have been cut away: there is only a hole, a black hole that should show teeth, but I suspect those have been removed as well. There is no blood – the wounds have healed – and as I zoom in even closer, what is left of the face appears on the high-def screen like melted wax.

I'm off the bed and I grab the scope. I'm thinking of the triple pay as I focus in on the Interim. The red dot lands squarely on its chest and I move it downwards until I find the back of its hand and I rest the laser on the QR code. I use the tracker pad to enlarge the dot until the red circle covers the entire code. I pull the trigger, and the image is frozen on the screen, capturing the data. I just have to double click and press *transmit* and the details will be sent to the police. The cops will be there in a matter of seconds. The Interim will be arrested and detained, not at the treatment centre – his escape has proven that he has the wrong personality profile for a mask. He'll be taken to the processing centre.

I'm trying to decide what to do, when there's movement in my peripheral vision, and I turn from the screen to the open door and the balcony.

There's a bird. It's landed on the metal balustrade, and it's watching me, its head at an angle. It's weird, because it's dark, and surely birds only come out in the daytime? It's a tiny thing, fragile and delicate. Defenceless. It fluffs up its feathers, and hops from one foot to another, and that's when I recognise it as a wren.

My finger hovers over the touchpad.

The Birds of Nagasaki

Spring came in with a flourish over the Easter holidays, festooning the cherry tree with frivolous white blossoms so suddenly that, even from this distance of thirty years, I remember it as having happened overnight. You and I were friends for those weeks you were home from school, the reluctance on your part at spending two weeks in the company of your little sister outweighed by relief at having escaped the torturous attention of your classmates. Even though you would not admit it, I think you were glad to have a playmate and a stooge, and we had a shared interest in the cherry tree, of course.

It was a large part of our childhood, in much the same way as sweets on a Saturday from the village shop and boiled eggs for Sunday tea: it was always there and, we assumed, always would be. It was a den and a fort, a headquarters and a castle. For a couple of weeks we forged a friendship of convenience, you and I, although our relationship never quite knew parity. You, older by two years, were always the captain, or the king, to my lieutenant or princess. Our games revolved around positions of power, and you would threaten me with a Chinese burn or a dead leg if I didn't play my role correctly. You were small for your age, smaller than I was, and you were made to suffer for it at school. Pigeon-chested, yours was a frail frame that jutted with bones. Your asthma contributed to your misfortune; even moderate exercise made you wheeze and reach for your inhaler. Your inability to take part in sport at school further singled you out as a target for the bullies, and you transferred your hatred to me in the form of petty torments: tiny but savage pinches up my arms and on the backs of my legs when no-one was looking.

For that time during the holidays, while Father was away and Mother sat at the kitchen table with stagnant eyes and a cloudy whisky glass, the cherry tree was our playground. The bench underneath acted as a ladder to its gnarled branches, and, cushioned with moss, these served as our climbing frame. You would urge me ever upwards, your delight at my alarm evident: your eyes would brighten and your usually pallid cheeks would flush, made rosy, until my fear would erupt and my snivelling begin to grate. You would allow me to clamber back down to earth, the tears on my cheeks mingling with the lichen stains on my palms as I tried to quell my terror.

It is dark like tar when I open my eyes and I wonder for a moment if I have truly opened them, or whether I am still asleep. I blink a few times, but nothing changes; there is no confirmation from my surroundings whether I am awake or asleep, or, for that matter, alive or dead. Then I hear the first familiar flutter and I know I am both alive and awake.

Father returned from his business trip just as the Easter holidays were drawing to a close. By then Mother was fraught and tired and the skin around her fingernails was red and raw from her continuous picking. The whisky bottle on the cocktail tray was almost empty. We always loved it when Father came home after working away. We had missed him, of course – the house was too big for just the three of us and there was no fun to be had without him. But it was the presents he would bring, the exotic gifts from far-off places, that we looked forward to most. It was almost as much fun as Christmas.

'Marcus!' he exclaimed, picking you up under the arms and – even though at twelve you were far too old for it – throwing you into the air and catching you again. Your small frame allowed you to be treated as though you were a younger child, and you detested this infantilisation of you. Then it would be my turn, and he always seemed to catch me more carefully, to hold on to me for a little bit longer. I was his favourite, and the narrowing of your eyes told me that you knew it.

Commercial flights had not long opened up to Japan at that time, and Father was ablaze with stories about the huge aeroplane and the elegant stewardesses who'd served him dainty morsels of raw fish and tiny glasses of saké. He lit a cigarette and further prolonged our anxious wait for our gifts with tales of the cherry blossom – *sakura* in Japanese, I now know – that filled the air above the streets with frothy clouds and a delicate scent, even more beautiful than our own cherry tree at the bottom of the garden. He told us of the tawdry neon signs, and of the ancient temples that were dotted about the city, incongruous against the glass and steel. He knew what he was doing and, just as we thought that we might burst with anticipation, he pulled a paper bag from his suitcase.

Mother had softened towards him by then, the bottle of duty-free whisky duly opened and poured, and her face displayed genuine delight when he presented her with a small ball of wood. She seemed to know what it was, and she held it in her palm and rubbed her thumb over the glossy surface. We peered at it, and on closer inspection we could see that the surface of the ball was carved, and the curve of the wood depicted the curled-up form of a rat, its tail coiled over and around its body, its small, hard eyes glossier than the rest of the wood.

For you he had a doll, a samurai warrior. Also carved from wood, the little man was the length of your hand and helmeted, with the armour picked out in painstakingly painted detail. He held a sword with a thin metal blade. Your disdain was evident; the doll was too babyish for a twelve-year-old, too feminine for a man-child. You deliberately discarded it on the table but Father didn't notice – he had already turned his attention to me.

He pulled from the bag a folded piece of blue silk, an intense cobalt which caught the light and shimmered slightly as he shook it out. A kimono, he explained, a traditional jacket that Japanese ladies wore. I stood still for a moment, trying to take in its beauty, and then he placed it on my shoulders. The sheen of the fabric belied its bulk, and I felt my shoulders sink under its weight.

'Give us a twirl, then,' Father said, and I complied, always happy to play my role of Daddy's girl. I swung around, enjoying the sensation of momentum as the kimono swung from my shoulders and caught the air, and that's when I heard you gasp.

'What?' I demanded. 'What is it?'

But you said nothing. I dragged the kimono from my shoulders and turned it around and that's when I saw for the first time what was on the back. Three cranes: white-feathered, soaring and suspended gracefully in flight, their delicate shapes repeated in gradually diminishing shadow form behind them. The needlework was exquisite, the edges of the wings picked out in detail, and here and there individual feathers were depicted in tiny stitches. Each bird wore a cap of crimson. It was the most beautiful thing I had ever seen.

The flutter is still there in the darkness. I lie for a moment, absorbing the familiar rustle. It is neither comforting nor distressing, but has become an indelible part of my existence. My eyes have now become more accustomed to the darkness, and a pale halo glows around the window, the faintest indication of an outdoor, moonlit world.

The next day – the penultimate day of the Easter holidays – we took up our places on the bench under the cherry tree.

We had brought our collection of paper birds with us, and they lay strewn on the grass around our feet. Daddy had told us about them; he'd been invited to dinner at the house of one of his Japanese colleagues, and his wife – who spoke no English but had beautiful, delicate hands – had showed him how to make tiny cranes out of squares of crisp paper. He demonstrated how to make the folds, encouraging us in our precision and symmetry. Our first attempts were clumsy and lopsided, the edges dull and worn and grubby from our efforts, but we persevered and gradually became more accomplished at scoring the folds with our fingernails until they were sharp and neat. Soon we had a whole flock of tiny birds, their wings folded carefully into their bodies, beaks jutting sharp as needles from their hard-edged heads. We took to perching the origami birds in the cherry tree, do you remember? We must have created dozens of them that day, and we arranged them on the branches, nestling them amongst the frothy blossom. The flowers were so abundant, so virulent, that the cranes were barely visible, the white paper camouflaged among the creamy blooms.

We'd known about the hole under the cherry tree for a little while, of course. We'd discovered it right at the start of the holidays when you'd invented a game that required me to lie on my front, the mossy ground springy beneath me, and for you to balance on my back, like a surfer, your shoes pressing into my shoulder blades. You'd insisted that I be the one to lie down – if I were to stand on your back it would be sure to cause an asthma attack – but you'd soon got bored and stepped down, and when I pushed myself up my hand went straight into the earth and found nothing but damp air.

The Birds of Nagasaki

The tree's roots stood proud of the ground, and had pushed their way through the mud like the limbs of a primeval beast. In the apex of two of the roots, the soil gave away to a cave-like structure, guarded from view by a rich cap of moss. We'd made an inspection of the hole that day, lying on our stomachs and poking sticks around in the darkness, stirring the loam-scented air. It had soon lost its novelty, though, and we'd thrown the sticks inside and covered it over with an old floorboard we found in the garage, and then dragged the bench over the top to keep it in place.

Now, however, I could see your interest in the tree-hole had been reignited. You'd already grown bored of the paper cranes and complained loudly of the paper cuts that criss-crossed your fingers. That familiar spark of cruelty flared in your eyes. When you made me stand up to help you drag the bench, scattering all the paper birds to the ground, and then kicked the floorboard aside, I knew what was going to happen. I should have run away then, but something told me that the consequences of doing so would be worse than what you were about to do to me.

The hole under the cherry tree was only a small space, but I meekly obeyed your order to climb into it; even though I was scared of the dark, I was more scared of what you'd do to me if I resisted. I wrapped my arms around my legs, and because I'd tucked my head into my chest to make myself as small as I could, a little bundle of limbs surrounded by dirt, I couldn't look up, couldn't see if there was any daylight penetrating the mossy lid. I tried not to cry, because I knew that would make you angry. The thing I remember most is the damp, organic smell of the earth, the feeling that the air and the soil were

201

becoming one and that I would be trapped in there forever, in that subterranean prison, unable to breathe.

The first movement around my head and on my shoulders made me think of rats, of my mother's piece of carved wood, with its sleek tail and glossy, vindictive eyes, but just as the panic was rising in my throat I felt the delicate touch of wings against my cheeks. I thought of moths, or beetles, or other winged creatures that might inhabit this underground space, but the wings were hard, and sharp, and there were dozens of them, catching in my hair. I grasped one and touched it with the fingers of my other hand. Even in my terror I was able to tell what it was. An origami bird.

I am no longer scared of the dark. I pull back the covers and feel my way to the window. The snow that came tonight started as small, delicate flakes that drifted, forlorn, then leapt suddenly upwards, like puppets on an unseen cord. I draw back the curtain and stand for a while. The snowflakes have grown larger, heavier, and as they fall they almost obscure the cherry tree, which is painted in watercolours against a cloud-sodden sky. Moonlight renders the snowflakes crystalline. People think that snow has no smell, that it's merely frozen water, and that water will only freeze if it's pure, untainted. But snowflakes are formed when ice crystals gather around miniscule pieces of dirt that have been transported to the atmosphere by the wind. They cluster together, growing bigger and bigger, allowing the contamination to spread. Snow is not as pure as people are led to believe.

*

The Birds of Nagasaki

A few times, you'd asked me if I wanted to swap my kimono for your samurai doll. 'Dolls,' you'd said, 'are for girls. Jackets can be for anyone.' Normally, I would have acquiesced: your two-year seniority gave you status, even if your diminutive stature didn't. But this time I held firm. The kimono was precious to me. I would shrug my arms into its sleeves and stand and stare at myself in the mirror, looking over my shoulder at the triptych of cranes that soared across my back, imagining them taking to the sky and gliding into oblivion. Then I would remove the kimono again and simply stroke the fabric, the weft of the silk slightly slubbed, the embroidery thread perfectly silvery smooth against the heavenly blue. It whispered of exotic places and I swore I could smell spices and oranges and smoke when I buried my nose in its folds. I knew that you coveted the kimono, but so did I, and for once I held out against your demands. Your reward to me was a row of bruises along my inner arms that bloomed grey, then purple, before settling a few days later into a sickly yellow.

It was your idea to hold the funeral. It was the very last day of the holidays, and the next day you were going to be put on a train and sent back to school. I would not see you until summer. By then your samurai doll was missing a leg and his head was set at a peculiar angle, and I knew that you'd damaged it on purpose, a petulant response to being given a toy you thought was beneath you.

'Best to put him out of his misery,' you'd said, and you bashed him against the trunk of the cherry tree until he fell to pieces, his head chipped, his limbs lying like twigs on the grass, his metal sword bent. The flock of paper birds we'd discarded there were gathered around like observers at a road accident. Your violence shocked me; you had always been cruel to me, but it was as though the months you'd spent away at boarding school had toughened you, instilled a dark side to your nature that I had not witnessed before.

'If we're going to have a funeral, it must be a proper one,' you'd said.

It was your idea that the samurai doll should be buried in a shroud.

It is cold at the bedroom window, but I don't turn away. I wrap my arms around myself – they are bruised, tender. The snowfall is heavier still, and as I watch the flakes become blossom, become feathers, become birds.

The kitchen shears cut easily through the dense weave of the silk, and they stuttered briefly only when they met a small resistance from the embroidered shadows. The three large cranes, their red-capped heads picked out in delicate, smooth stitches, formed the centrepiece of the shroud. I had cried when you'd told me what you were going to do. I had begged you not to, had even threatened to go to Father and tell him what you were planning, but I could see in the coldness of your eyes, in the hard jut of your jaw, that you would have your way. There was no use fighting you – you had proven that you would always beat me – so I gave in to the inevitable. In an act of obscene cruelty, you made me take the kimono from my drawer and hand it to you, a sacrifice. Do you remember? You smiled then, and that familiar flush rose on your cheeks, your eyes flickering with anticipation.

The Birds of Nagasaki

You wrapped the samurai in the square of fabric, your movements quick and sharp and vindictive as you secured the fabric with elastic bands, no regard shown for the gravity of the act or the solemnity of the occasion. A paper cut reopened on your finger with the abruptness of your actions. A drop of blood fell and blossomed maroon against the cobalt.

The blizzard has by now obscured the cherry tree, and instead I allow my gaze to fall to the windowsill. The flutter of paper has manifested itself into a bird, the folds sharp, the edges crisp. I cross to the mantelpiece and place the origami crane there, at random, amidst the flock of hundreds of identical birds that have appeared with increasing frequency over the last thirty years. Some have grown dull with age, but the more recent ones are still bright and rigid. They have started to cascade from the shelf, and a flock of them has gathered on the floor, threatening to spread and fill the room.

'Help me, then,' you demanded, and I edged forward, leaning into the trench alongside you. You'd attempted to throw the samurai to the bottom of the hole, but the shroud had snagged on a rogue root. The stick you'd found to dislodge the blue silk wasn't long enough, and you were stretching, trying to make it reach. You'd planned to inter the little warrior doll in the tree-hole, and cover him up with a coating of soil. To create a burial chamber which would be the samurai's final resting place, we would pull the floorboard over the hole and rest the bench on top. I was glad: that would mean that you could no longer force me into that terrible dark jail.

I could tell that your temper was fraying. Once again your small stature meant that you couldn't get what you wanted: you couldn't reach the samurai to dislodge it from the root and you couldn't stand the thought that something had triumphed over you. I suggested that I might climb into the tree-hole, somehow thinking that if I could pick up the bundle I could salvage the square of silk, could stitch the cranes back into the kimono and make it whole again. I knew that this would mean the terror of being underground, and the possibility that you would shut me in again, to share a resting place with the samurai, but my offer was driven by desperation, and an overwhelming desire to mend the desecrated kimono.

I think my suggestion made you rethink the situation; you were in charge, and it was your responsibility to bury the samurai. You were cautious at first, as you climbed down, holding on to the tree's roots as you guided your legs in. The space was small – you hadn't anticipated how small – and I could hear your voice, muffled, as you cursed. You had to manoeuvre awkwardly in order to bend over to reach the bundle, and you seemed to become jammed in the space, only the ridge of your spine visible through your white shirt.

The floorboard wasn't heavy, and – with my superior strength – I was able to haul it into place quite easily. I had to drag the bench on top of it. Your fear was evident in your shouts – shouts that were diminished after I arranged handfuls of moss over the floorboard, careful to block any gaps that might allow the ingress of air. Gradually, your voice subsided, and your protestations turned to begging, and then to occasional laboured wheezing. I don't know how long I sat there on the bench, my hands occupied with the scoring and folding of crisp white paper squares. It must have been hours, until eventually the light started to fade.

The snow that came that night was unexpected: a freak snowstorm that hadn't been anticipated by the weatherman, and so no warning had been given. We awoke the next day to a perfect white blanket that lay pristine and unsullied and covered the entire garden. It had somehow even encroached onto the patch of ground under the cherry tree, rendering the floorboard invisible, and the bench merely a lumpen silhouette.

Our parents had been up all night, searching the lane for you, calling the neighbours and giving descriptions to the police of the blue car I reported having seen loitering outside our gate. Of course, the snowfall hampered their efforts, and you never did return to school. You were never found.

When I am ready, I return to my bed. My shivering tells me it's getting cold, much colder than before. I can clearly make out the luminescence ringing the space where the window is, brighter now, the moonlight intensified by the thick layer of snow that covers the ground.

Then I wait. I wait for the loamy scent of soil and decaying leaf matter to reach my nostrils, and for the air around me to become oppressive with damp. I wait to hear the soft slither of the sheets being drawn back as you slide into bed next to me, and your hoarse, wheezing rasp. *Sakura, sakura, sakura.* Your tiny fingers will be icy and still cloaked in earth as they pinch at my skin in the dark.

Some of these stories have previously appeared in print, as follows:

'Jutland' © 2019, originally published as a chapbook by Nightjar Press.

'Badgerface' © 2018, originally published in *The Lonely Crowd Issue Ten*, edited by John Lavin, and subsequently in *Best British Short Stories 2019*, edited by Nicholas Royle (Salt Publishing).

'The Pickling Jar' © 2019, originally published in *The Ghastling No. 9*, edited by Rebecca Parfitt.

'Resting Bitch Face' © 2020, originally published in *Black Static 76* edited by Andy Cox (TTA Press).

'Cortona' © 2019, originally published in *'Make a Wish, Keep the Wish Secret,'* (TSS Publishing).

'The Devil of Timanfaya' © 2019, originally published in *The Shadow Booth Vol. 4*, edited by Dan Coxon.

'Wretched' © 2020, originally published in *The New Abject* edited by Sarah Eyre and Ra Page (Comma Press).

'The Birds of Nagasaki' © 2020 originally published in *Uncertainties IV*, edited by Timothy J. Jarvis (Swan River Press).

All other stories are original to this collection.

Acknowledgements

My thanks go to the team at Dead Ink – Nathan Connolly, Jordan Taylor-Jones and Laura Jones – for getting this book out into the world, and also to Ella Chappell for her superb editing skills.

I am grateful to Dr Adam Crothers, Special Collections Assistant at the Library of St John's College, Cambridge, for his help in seeking permission to include the quotation from the Hugh Sykes Davies poem in the epigraph.

Several of these stories have previously appeared in print, and my thanks go to the editors of those publications, many of whom expended considerable time and effort on working with me to improve my efforts.

Writing can be a solitary business, so heartfelt thanks must also go to Justine Bothwick, Johnny Mains, Anna Vaught and Michael Walters – dear friends and writers who have read and commented on these stories, and provided enormous quantities of support and cheerleading. You are the best.

And once again, thanks to Dom for his eternal patience and support, and to Ted, Ben and Florence who still persist in asking, 'When can I read your stories?' even though for whom the answer is always, 'When you're a bit older.'

About the Author

Lucie McKnight Hardy grew up in West Wales and is a Welsh speaker. She has also lived in Liverpool, Cardiff, Zurich and Bradford, and is now settled in Herefordshire with her family. Her debut novel, *Water Shall Refuse Them*, was published by Dead Ink in 2019.

About Dead Ink

Supported by Arts Council England, we're focussed
on developing the careers of new
and emerging authors.

Our readers form an integral part of our team.
You don't simply buy a Dead Ink book,
you invest in the authors and the books you love.

You can keep up to date with the latest Dead Ink
events, workshops, releases and calls for
submissions by signing up to our mailing
list or our Patreon.

deadinkbooks.com
@deadinkbooks
patreon.com/deadinkbooks